49

# MEMOIR

WRITTEN DURING

# A SURVEY OF THE WATLING STREET,

FROM THE TEES TO THE SCOTCH BORDER,

IN THE YEARS 1850 AND 1851,

MADE BY DIRECTION OF

## HIS GRACE THE DUKE OF NORTHUMBERLAND,

ON THE OCCASION OF THE MEETING OF THE ARCHÆOLOGICAL INSTITUTE,
AT NEWCASTLE-UPON-TYNE.

## By HENRY MACLAUCHLAN.

LONDON:
PUBLISHED AT THE OFFICE OF THE ARCHÆOLOGICAL INSTITUTE,
26 SUFFOLK STREET, PALL MALL.
MDCCCLII.

G.A.Eng. roads x° 137

LONDON :
BRADBURY AND EVANS, PRINTERS, WHITEFRIARS.

TO

HIS GRACE THE DUKE OF NORTHUMBERLAND,

UNDER WHOSE AUSPICES AND BY WHOSE MUNIFICENCE

THE SURVEY OF THE ROMAN ROAD FROM THE RIVER SWALE TO THE SCOTCH BORDER

WAS UNDERTAKEN AND ACCOMPLISHED,

This Memoir is Dedicated.

# MEMOIR WRITTEN DURING A SURVEY OF THE WATLING STREET,

FROM THE TEES TO THE SCOTCH BORDER, IN THE YEARS 1850 AND 1851.

## BY HENRY MACLAUCHLAN.

THE course of the Roman road, to which these notes refer, is nearly N.W. from Pierse Bridge[1] on the Tees, to Chew Green on the Coquet, a distance of 69 miles. Unlike many Roman works of the same age, it is straight in no part for any great distance, though the line might often have been made so; still, it has been laid out generally so as to take advantage of the nature of the ground.

The best general view of the line may be had from the following conspicuous heights, which probably were used originally to lay out the line, and from having beacons on them (with one exception),may have served also for conveying signals: *Brusselton, Brandon Down, Pontop Pike, Stagshaw Bank, Fourlaws,* and *Thirlmoor.* On this line there are eight Roman stations, varying from *four* acres in size in the northern or Ottadini country, to *eight* in that of the Brigantes. These stations, with the exception of Chew Green, seem all to have been inclosed by walls of masonry: they are, *Pierse Bridge, Binchester, Lanchester, Ebchester, Corbridge, Risingham, Rochester,* and *Chew Green.* In no case are these stations more than 100 yards from the road, and generally not more than as many feet. There are other Roman camps near the line, much larger than the stations, and at a greater distance in some cases, but none a mile from the road. Besides these, are other small ancient camps, about the size of an acre or less: these are not so near the road, and apparently not connected with it.

The map has been constructed on the published triangulation of the Ordnance Survey,[2] and laid down to a scale of two inches to a mile. The maps of the stations and camps have been constructed to an uniform and larger scale of eight chains to an inch, by means of chain measurements; and the detail of the intervening portions of the line of the Watling Street by traverse with a theodolite, with occasional reference to the maps of the Tithe Office, through the kindness of Major Dawson of the Royal Engineers. Each point in the triangulation has been calculated to the meridian, and its perpendicular, of the station on Burley Moor, from the

---

[1] The map of that part of the Watling-street, between the Swale and the Tees, has been added from a survey made in 1848, the notes to which were published in the Journal of the Archæological Institute, No. 23. The whole line from the Swale to the Cheviots has been lithographed on six sheets to which reference will be found in the text.

[2] Ordnance Trigonometrical Survey vol. iii., p. 339.

data given in the volumes of the Survey. Hence the distances between any two Roman stations has been ascertained from calculation, and not by measurement with the chain; and the inflections of the road determined by small triangles running along the line.[3]

In a former paper we offered a conjecture that the nearness to each other of the three stations Catterick, Greta Bridge, and Pierse Bridge, with other Roman works of small posts within the triangle, would lead to a conclusion that there was some considerable force to control within the space enclosed, and which might point to the people occupying the entrenchments at Stanwick. The size of Catterick (see Map-Sheet, No. 1) and Pierse Bridge also is greater than any other of the stations in passing to the northward, particularly of the latter, about the extent of which there can be no doubt. How far its size may entitle it to the designation of the *Magis* in the Notitia, is left for others to consider; but both Horsley and Hodgson, the Northumbrian historian, place *Magis* at Pierse Bridge. Pierse Bridge contains about 8¾ acres within the *walls*, the outline of which, however, is very imperfectly made out. The Watling Street runs within about two hundred yards of the station, on the east side of it, and with which it was connected by a road, the traces of which may be yet observed in dry weather.[4] (See Map-Sheet, No. 2.)

About three hundred yards from the Tees, our line joins the turnpike road to Auckland, and continues along it with very little deviation, first on one side, and then on the other, till we arrive at Legs Cross, where there is a slight trace of an entrenchment running nearly at right angles to the road; but whether thrown up for agricultural or warlike purposes cannot now be confidently stated. About this spot the great Whynstone dyke crosses the way. The stones at Legs Cross are formed of the basaltic rocks, and were they more flat than they are, we should hazard a British origin for the ancient memorial —(*Llech*). About ten furlongs beyond the Cross we come to the Royal Oak, where for about one hundred and fifty yards the public way ceases to coincide with the Watling Street,[5] but the

[3] It will be obvious that such a survey could not be carried through a country without the assistance of the landed proprietors, and in Northumberland we experienced that of his Grace, through his agents; that of Lord Redesdale, through Mr. Lawson; Mr. Riddel of Swinburne Castle; and Mr. Grey of Dilston Hall. In the county of Durham we have to acknowledge that of the Lord Bishop, with the free use of his map of Binchester, through his secretary Mr. Griesley. Many others of equal kindness deserve our warmest thanks, among whom we may mention the clergy generally, and Mr. James Raine of Durham in particular. In the derivation of names of places, we have to acknowledge the assistance of Mr. John Just, of Bury, Lancashire.

[4] Mr. Denham points out several rude stone coffins, and bones, projecting from the bank of the river Tees, exposed as the earth is washed away by the river; and one projecting from the face of a quarry at Carlbury, on the west of the road, to be seen as you pass by. The camp at Pierse Bridge is ten miles two furlongs from Cataractonium, in a straight line; and ten miles three furlongs by the Watling-street.

[5] Many antiquaries have given derivations of watling; perhaps it may be from the Anglo-Saxon—*watel*, to cover, from the stone of the Roman road forming a *roof*, or *cover*, to throw off the water. Horsley says, "I know not whether the name *watling* street be derived from the *winding* nature of it."—Brit. Rom., p. 387. Stukeley says, "thus: *Watling* Street tending directly to Ireland no doubt was called the Irish road, that is the *Gathelian* road, *Gathelian* street, whence our present word *Wales*, from *Gauls, warden* from *guardian*," &c. —Itinerarium Curiosum, p. 105.

traces are very evident, and the straight line nearly continuous. Proceeding, we reach the high ground at Brusselton, and our road runs about two hundred yards on the east of the Gazebo, called the Folly, which was fixed in the trigonometrical survey, and is about six hundred and eighty feet above the sea.

From this elevated spot there is a magnificent view, and some traces of an outpost were expected at a point so commanding. Not finding them, it was conjectured that the distant camp at Shackerton might possibly have served such a purpose, to which its nearly right-lined and rectangular shape make it eligible. Shakerton,⁶ or Shackleton, Hill, or, as it is now better known, Windmill Hill, is a woody knoll, about five furlongs on the west of Redworth, in the parish of Heighington, and about 2½ miles S.E. of the Watling Street at Brusselton Folly. Its area is about ¼ acre. It is· surrounded on the west side by three ramparts, the two outer of which are extended on the east so as to enclose a small space, giving the camp that peculiar ·character which has entitled it to be considered of Danish origin, and approaching the form of that at Castle Hills, on the Swale; Sedberg, on the Rotha; and Hornby, on the Lune; which have been considered either Saxon or Danish. This remarkable shape, however, will not prevent the supposition that the camp had been originally formed by Roman, or even British people; and its name, Shackerton, may possibly be only a corruption of *uchel-don* (*upper*, or *lofty, camp*—Brit.): which name will be appropriate, whether applied to its particular situation, or relatively to 'Pierse Bridge and Binchester, between which it would form a suitable outpost or signal station. In the latter case, the outwork attached, to which reference has been made, must have been added subsequently.' (See Map-Sheet, No. 2.)

The area given above will only include the plain surface on the summit; the whole, including the three ramparts, may be about 3¼ acres. There is a building near the centre on the top, which was once a windmill, it is said; which was afterwards turned into a gazebo, or summerhouse; and now stands a ruin, surrounded by lofty trees and wood, which render any estimate of a true conception of the ground rather difficult.

⁶ The agent of the proprietor asserts, that he has seen a deed of great antiquity in which the name is spelt *Shackerton*.

⁷ "It is wound round with three distinct terraces, and it is thought to be the remains of a Danish fort; the mount bearing an exact similitude to those of the more northern parts of this island, where the Danes were stationed for many years. It is the only monument we have observed of that people between Tyne and Tees." —Hutchinson. "From its lofty elevation, and the wide prospect from its summit, it is well calculated for a post of observation; but there is no evidence to confirm Hutchinson's supposition."—Mackenzie's Hist. Durham, vol. ii., p. 169. Though there is so fine a view from Brusselton, it is principally to the northward and west-ward, the breadth and nearly equal height between Legs Cross and it preventing a view into both the valley of Tees and Weardale from the same spot. This place will interest the geologist as well as the antiquary, for it is on this broad ridge that the newer magnesian limestone overlies unconformably the strata of the coal measures, the former dipping gently to the south, and the latter more rapidly to the north. How far this upthrow of the coal is occasioned by igneous rocks below is for the geologist to speculate on; but it is of short continuance, and probably does not extend far beyond the course of the Gaunless, where a gentle rise of the coal measures to the north-west sets on.

At Brusselton Folly, a view of the camp at Binchester is first obtained over Bishop Auckland, and it is probable the road would have been continued in a straight line but for the advantages to be gained in passing the river Gaunless at a very favourable spot, where it is free from those deep sinuosities for which it is remarkable. Before we reach this spot, however, it is necessary to notice an ancient way crossing the Watling Street at right angles, called Hummerbeck Lane, presumed to be that referred to by Hutchinson, as passing "by Streatham and between Staindrop and West Auckland, a little to the southward of the present turnpike road, and so to the foot of Bildershaw Hill, where it is joined to the great Roman road from Pierse Bridge to Binchester."—(His. Dur., vol. iii.p. 297.)

Hummerbeck Lane crosses the Watling Street at Burn House, a small cottage, and keeping the dry ground above the reach of the Gaunless, runs in an even curve towards St. Andrew's Auckland. It has much the appearance of a Roman way, though much less characteristic than the Watling Street.[8]  Crossing the Gaunless at Fielding Bridge, about 130 yards on the east of the present bridge, so as to clear a small rill which falls in on the east of it, the road runs very nearly straight to Bishop Auckland, the present road coinciding very nearly with the original line which may be seen at intervals by its ruined elevation.

If this be true it will have entered the town by Newgate, though it seems probable that the houses on the east side are likely to stand on the west side of the line, and thus the road will have entered the market-place between the church and the market-house; this is best observed from Brusselton Hill.

We may observe here what has been noticed before, that, in making the road, the general line through the country having been decided on, no particular care was taken to carry forward a straight line over a hill, as in the Fosse Way, and other Roman lines, but the course was made straight from one eminence to another, and then a new direction taken forward to the next rising ground; unless, as in the case of crossing the Gaunless, some considerable object was to be gained by a deviation.

No traces whatever of the road can be discerned through Bishop Auckland to Binchester, though an examination of the declivity to the Gaunless will show that it could not conveniently have passed further to the eastward than has been described. To point out its probable course it will be necessary to examine Binchester, and the course of the river Wear.

Binchester is generally allowed "to be the Vinovium of Antoninus, and the Binovium of Ptolemy."[9]  Its geological position seems to be in a

---

[8] The farmer, at New Moors Pottery, "hacked up the stones of the road across his farm to build a cottage with," and points out its course distinctly marked by the remaining stones. This is about a mile west of Hummerbeck Bridge, West Auckland. Towards the east this road is pointed out as a stone causeway, about four feet wide, by Timothy and Thomas Brown, old residents at the Deanery Farm, St. Andrew's Auckland; first on one side of the road and then on the other, about 200 yards south of the Deanery farm-house. From Fielding Bridge it is a bridle way to South Auckland, and not being traceable further than the Darlington road, is presumed to have taken its course towards Durham and Chester-le-Street.

[9] Hutchinson says, "by Antiquarians of the first character said to be the Vinovium of Antoninus, and the Binovium

synclinal line, or trough, of the coal strata, as may be seen by the gentle dip at Newfield towards the south, and the dip to the north by the Gaunless at the castle. It appears almost an island in the valley of the Wear, and a rise of about thirty feet above the floor of the great floods would probably now render it so. The surface is covered with *diluvium*, and to such a depth apparently, that, situated as it is, where the river made nearly a right angle in its general course, and at the same time received the Gaunless, it seems not impossible, that it is entirely composed of it. From this it will be seen, that Binchester was a place of great strength naturally, and though the Roman stationary camp was comparatively small, there was ample room on the spot for an extensive entrenchment. From the remains at present existing it is not easy to imagine the exact size of the station. (See Map-Sheet, No. 2.)

The whole of the N.E. front is traceable, and about half of the N.W. and S.E. fronts; on this assumption the fortress will have been a right-angled parallelogram, with the N.E. and S.W. fronts about 214 yards in length, and the N.W. and S.E. fronts about 160 yards. This would give an area of about seven acres. It would appear, that the Watling Street ran through the two latter fronts of the station, not approaching the S.E., or leaving the N.W. perpendicularly to each front, but deviating nearly the same (about three degrees) in each instance, and in both cases uniformly towards the north; something similar to Catterick. This is imagined from what is taken to be the road as it approaches the S.E. front from the precipice, down which declivity the ruins are still to be seen, which it is believed others have taken for "the south-west corner of the vallum."[1]

On examination it will be seen, that the curve formed in the vallum-like ridge, which is in the narrow strip of plantation, which divides the lawn from the large field, is of larger radius than such earthworks were generally formed of; and that the large stones mentioned may have been the pavement of the road, the stones of which in some instances were larger than a man could lift.

The radius which struck the curve was about 100 yards in length, and a tangent to it at the spot, where it has been destroyed by the falling of the cliff, would run in the direction of the bridge in the Park, too far to the eastward to hit the market-place, where we left the road; but if we allow the curve to have continued but a little further, which probably it did, our road would take the tangent line to the place desired. In this case it will be necessary to conceive the Wear to have changed its course in the lapse of centuries; which an examination of the ancient bed of the stream near the Flats Farm-house, and the several water-marks

of Ptolemy." Binovium, Vinovium, or Vinovia, perhaps may be derived from *Bann — lofty, tall;* or *Gwynn—suitable, pleasant, fair; y-Vann;* either very appropriate, and probably the signification of other Roman stations so commencing : and with the addition, in this instance, of *via,* a Latin word we may easily conceive the Brigantes to have adopted, when forced by the legionaries to make the road, Vann-y-Via.

[1] "In the break of the bank at the south-west corner, the foundations of the vallum are laid open, consisting of very large blocks of stone laid transversely." —Hutchinson's Hist. Durham, vol. iii., p 429.

across the level ground on the east, will abundantly justify. The direction from the market-house will have been obliquely down the road called the Wear-chair,[2] the upper part of which is somewhat lower than the ground on each side of it.

It must be confessed that there is little now remaining to carry out this line of road, but on careful examination of the ground, we cannot assign any other so probable. Should it be required to point out the next likely course, according with the present bed of the river, we might select an oblique descent from the market-place, near the park wall, along the present road by Jock's Row, and up the precipice, by a singular water-worn projection, having all the appearance of an artificial structure; for it does not seem probable that the more natural and beautiful curve down the present approach to the castle, over the bridge and to Binchester, up the gradual ascent, about 170 yards on the east of the present road, would have accorded with Roman military engineering. It may be added that the bowling-green at the castle has much the appearance of a camp.

Supposing the construction of the station to have been as described, and a gateway in the centre of each front, which seems probable, with streets passing from these gates through the work at right angles to each other, the hypocaust will have been under the corner building at the south angle.

Its interior dimensions are, length 22 feet, breadth 16 feet, and height 4½ feet. Add to the breadth, a division wall of three feet, in which are three arched openings, the centre one the largest, and also 4 feet for an entrance arched passage, at the end of which is a flight of five steps, and we have the size of the building in the interior; the thickness of the outer wall is not visible.[3]

There are eleven supporting pillars in one way, and eight in the other, in rows. The large tiles on the top of the pillars have the workman's marks on the under side. The impress, of which reduced

---

[2] This word, which is used at Newcastle-on-Tyne, as well as here, at Lincoln (the Mayor's chair), and at Durham, for a street or lane, is said to be a corruption of *shire*, that *which divides*, a *boundary*. Chare, s. a narrow lane or alley, less than a street. Of these there are several in Newcastle, particularly on the Quay side. Sax. *cerra*, via flexio, diverticulum; from *cyrran*, to turn; a chare being a turning from some superior street. So, a narrow street, in reference to its opening into a wide one, is called a turning in London, and a *wynd* in Edinburgh. Hence, too, a *char* woman is a woman for a *turn*, and a door a-*jar*, is a door on a *turn*.—Brockett's Glossary, vol. i., p. 88.

[3] "The remains of a Roman hypocaust, or bath were discovered (about 1815) here." (Binchester). "It is a small subterranean apartment, the descent to which is by a flight of steps; and it is intersected by regular ranges of brick pillars, about eight inches square, fifteen or sixteen inches apart, and nearly five feet high. The first floor above the pillars is formed by large square tiles, the four corners of each of which rest on the corners of four of the pillars; and these tiles are covered by a second floor of strong mortar and gravel. The remains of the flues for heating the superincumbent apartments are still visible."—Mackenzie's Hist. Durham, vol. ii., p. 304. Mr. Peter Fair, bookseller, of Bishop Auckland, was present when the hypocaust was discovered, which was by the striking of a plough against the wall of it. The passage and flight of steps, he states, were built by the proprietor, and the centre arch enlarged to allow of easy ingress. The mortar used in this part of the structure is not Roman (Mr. Bruce). The mansion is said to have been thrown down in 1835. To Mr. Fair and Mr. Peacock, we were much indebted for our information at Binchester; particularly to the latter, whose information extended along the Watling-street both to the north and south of Bishop Auckland.

representations are here given, measures 7 inches by 1½ inch. The letters are raised. The wall of the rampart is only visible in one place, the facing

MARKS ON ROMAN TILES, BINCHESTER.

stones of which have been removed; and at this spot the height of the rampart above the broad ditch is about 12 feet. The ditch has been broad, perhaps the same as at Lanchester, above sixty feet.

It seems probable that there was a way towards the coast from Binchester, and some may fancy they can trace a dyke running from the north-west gate, along the road towards Newfield; first on the east side, and then on the west, near Belburn Brook, ascending near the road, and running on the west side of it as far as the Newfield Brook, where the road turns to the east towards Bier's Green. Beyond this no trace may be seen, but about 350 yards before we reach the cross roads on the hill, there is a heap of stones in the road, having much the appearance of an ancient tumulus, so that a road possibly ran this way, by Bier's Green to the sea side. There is not the smallest trace of the Watling Street out of the north-west gate, towards the river Wear and Hunwick, but its course is so clear on the Hunwick side, and runs so nearly in a line with the gate we have assumed, that there can be no doubt of the line it took between Binchester[4] and the river Wear. Binchester is nine miles four furlongs from Pierse Bridge station, in a straight line, and nine miles six furlongs by the Watling Street.

The Roman Way continues visible as it ascends from the river Wear, and at the distance of about 1000 yards from it enters a blind lane, which it follows very obscurely for a short distance, and passes about 200 yards below the church at Hunwick. A little farther, it appears to enter the lane leading to Helmington Hall, and continues along it as far as the spot where the road turns off to the westward. The cottage and garden on the west side are on it, and its traces are clearly to be seen down to the brook at Helmington Hall, both at the cottage and in the field at the back of it. At the Hall the line is somewhat on the western edge of the road, as it ascends from the bridge, and continues along the course of the road to Willington, its raised bank being seen sometimes on one side and sometimes on the other of the present lane. At Willington Burn the

---

[4] " Binchester, in very early times, gave name to the resident family, and continued their property till the year 1420, when Ralph, Earl of Westmoreland, purchased it of Robert Bynchester, and it was part of the forfeitures of the unfortunate Earl : soon after which event this beautiful place was purchased by the family of Wren."—Hutchinson's Hist. Durham, vol. iii., p. 431. The last of the Wrens had an only daughter, who was married to a Mr. Lyon, who had sons, John and Charles ; the eldest succeeded him in the Hetton property, and his brother Charles at Binchester, who sold the property to the Bishop of Durham (Van Mildert), who took down the mansion. Hutchinson says it was " a fine old building of the style used in Queen Elizabeth's time, composed of a centre and two wings, the south wing having a noble semicircular window projected from a bracket; the north wing was modernised; the hall furnished with old armour and antiquities found on the spot ; " these are all dispersed no one knows where.

present road turns to the eastward, and the Watling Street continues straight across the burn, its remains being very visible on each side the brook.

On the north bank of the stream, so much of the remains exist as to have the appearance of a tumulus, and from this spot a Roman Way runs off in a straight line, passing close in front of Hollin Hall, in rear of West Park Farm-house, over the brook, where it is very visible, and thence obscurely under the cottage near Stockley Farm-house, to the high part of Stockley Pasture,[5] where are extensive ruins of what was once (within the memory of man) Stockley village, and where seem, from the position and shape of the ground, to be faint traces of a Roman camp,[6] of small dimensions. As we near the burn, a mound in the line of the way has been planted, which is either a perfect remain of what the road originally was along its whole line, or else a tumulus. As usual, there are but few vestiges of the road in the precipitous banks, but on the east side the stream are some stones, which perhaps formed a part of the line.

A short distance from the brook it enters the present road to Durham, in the village of Brancepeth; and being at first on the south side it crosses the turnpike road diagonally apparently, and leaves it where the present road makes a slight inclination to the southward. It has lately been dug up in one of the Littlewhite fields, along which it is still visible some distance north of Scripton House. It is presumed that this road leads to Chester-le-Street: the line points to the west of Durham, and so far seems to be a straight line from Willington to Brancepeth.[7] Returning to Willington Burn, the Watling Street continues straight across the burn,[8] below Milkinghope Farm, where its ridge is visible in the burn as well as in the fields; but as it gains the summit of Milkinghope Bank, it bears a little to the westward, and thence, on the east side of a fence, straight to Okenshaw Farm, the house of which it passes about 110 yards on the west of it, and crosses the road on the west of a large pond in it. As the line descends the hill to the Stockley Brook it is almost imperceptible, but is seen large and well-defined on each side of the brook, and may be traced

[5] This must be the road which Dr. Hunter traced till he " lost it in Brancepeth Park," the course above described being across what is called the *West Park*.

[6] The importance of this pass to the southward gave rise most likely to the origin of Brancepeth Castle. " Dr. Hunter told me, he had observed a military way going off from Watling Street near this place, which he supposed went to Chester-on-the-Street, between Durham and Newcastle; he traced it to Brancepeth Park, but could find it no further."—Horsley, Brit. Rom.

[7] Much conjecture has been formed as to the origin of the name Brancepeth, and a story is still related of a wild boar that infested the woods below Brandon Hill, and after causing much terror was destroyed. Hutchinson mentions the tradition.—Hist. Durham, vol. iii., p. 376. Whatever credit should be attached to this part of the origin of the name, there can be little doubt that *peth* was derived from the Roman road, for we find it used, as we shall see, in other places.

[8] In the field above this place, called High Thornfield, the old farmer, Robert Heron, points out very faint traces of a circular entrenchment of about an acre; and relates that, about ten years ago, the servants picked up some glass beads when the spot was first under the plough. It was probably a British camp. Its ancient name may have been preserved in that of the adjacent farm now known as *Stonechester*, where it is stated, however, that coins have been found. The inclosure of *Stonechester* took place about 1757, it is said. Hume had it from 1807 to 1830; he never saw or heard of any banks cast up, nor heard of any coins found. He sold it to Wilkinson, who states the same.

in the uncultivated parts of Weather-hill Farm, passing about 45 yards on the east of the house, and, gaining the summit, bears a little to the eastward, sufficient to clear the top of a deep ravine on the east, which ravine terminates in the road from Woolley to Brancepeth. Proceeding across West Brandon Farm, it may be indistinctly traced in the second field from the road, by the dryness of the pasture and the rushes growing on each side of it, by the stones ploughed up further on, and by the evidence of the farmer, rendering it certain that it crosses the road over Brandon Hill about 615 yards to the west of the mound[9] on which the Ordnance Trigonometrical Station is placed, which is 875 feet above the sea. The Watling would not be so well ascertained here, if it were not for the perfect state in which it is found about 550 yards beyond this road as it descends across the Hill-house Farm; in one part, where the plough has never been, the ridge seems perfect with the exception of the top-stones.

On a commanding spot, about 220 yards from our line, is a knoll called Brimmy, or Broomy Castle. It seems to have been latterly a walled building, a slight trace of which only now remains. It may have been about 30 feet in diameter, and has the appearance of having been a tumulus, or post of observation. As the line approaches the declivity of Ragspeth Wood it becomes less distinct, but within is clearly to be traced, taking advantage, apparently, of a natural ridge in the steep declivity, and descending the hill against the course of the stream below, so as to break the rapidity of the fall, assuming, by so doing, a new course to the westward, at an angle of 105°; a feature unexampled in any other part of its course.

When the ground is examined on each side of this great angle, the reason for its adoption will be evident: the two streams, the Stockley Beck and the intricate course of the Derness are thus passed after their affluents have fallen in, and all the wet ground, and the necessity for bridges which would have been otherwise requisite, avoided: this is particularly applicable to the Derness. When this is considered, with the keeping clear of the ravine on the east between these two streams, and the dry and gentle ascent onwards to Hugh Farm, the prudence of the line will be admitted. Descending Ragspeth Wood,[1] our line crosses the stream about 100 yards below the junction of the brooks, and where the river assumes the name of Derness, or Durness; perhaps so called from its dark and obscure course, rendered so in some measure by the precipitous nature of the wood immediately on the south of it. (Dwfr, water— and nos, night, or darkness. Brit.) Proceeding past Hugh Farm in a

---

[9] This mound has been supposed to have been formed artificially, as a place of sepulture, but looks more like rubbish from a quarry, close to it, than anything else. Hutchinson says, "On the crown of Brandon Hill, which is a very lofty eminence, commanding an extensive prospect on every side, is a remarkable tumulus, or mount of an oblong figure, 120 paces in circumference of the base, and now in height about twenty-four perpendicular feet. If this were erected for a beacon, it is a most conspicuous station; if it covers some hero who fell in battle, it denotes the resting-place of a person of high distinction, from its magnitude." —Hist. Durham, vol. iii., p. 386.

[1] Probably Ragspeth may be a corruption of Hag's-peth, so called from the very formidable appearance the road makes as a dyke in the wood; as the term Grimsdyke is applied in other similar cases. A farm near is called Hag's House.

gentle curve, our line crosses the road to Ash, about three-quarters of a mile on the west of that village; and about half a mile on the south-west is an entrenchment bearing the quadrangular form of a Roman camp, with the foundations of a castle, or strong stone building, near the middle of it, about which history affords us little information. It stands on Rowley Farm, between the Priest's and Rowley Beck, and so situated as to command a view of the Watling Street from Brandon Down towards Lanchester, so as to leave but a small part of the line unseen between it and the station at Lanchester, from which it is about three miles. (See Map-Sheet, No. 3.)

Though the ancient entrenchment appears to have been much altered in the improvements about the subsequent castle, such as deepening the ditch for water, and extending it at the north-east angle so as to form a small lake, sufficient of the Roman character remains to make it probable it was a camp of observation, though larger than those usually found along the Way. Its length is about 220 yards, and breadth 145, with an entrance on the south and another on the west, which last seems to have been altered to a more modern approach. Its area is about six acres. About 80 yards west of this last-mentioned entrance, was a tumulus, 21 feet by 12 feet, of an oval form, about 9 feet in height, and found, when opened by the farmer, about eleven years since (1840), to contain an arched hollow space, about 4 feet high and as many wide, containing ashes about 4 inches deep at the bottom, but no bones; these were scattered to the winds, and only a few fragments of bricks, of which the arch was made, remain to show of what the tomb was constructed. This tumulus, the form of the work, which is disproportionate to the size of the building within, and the name Rowley, which is probably only another name for *rah*, or *raw*, (British for a *camp*), when taken together, make it probable the entrenchment was originally a Roman work. The name it bears, *Castle Steads*, is not sufficient, perhaps, to weigh with the above, though familiar to places on the line of Roman wall. The foundations within the camp comprise a small space, only about 95 feet by 75, with a recess on the north as of a doorway, and a stone remaining which seems to have been the head of a window of two pointed lights, supposed, by some conversant with the subject, to indicate the style of the 13th century.

Coeval with this building seemingly, about 50 yards south of the camp, is a small enclosure about 76 yards square, called the *Chapel Garth*, in which are the foundations of a small building, about 20 yards by 10 yards, traditionally said to have been a place of worship, and old people have heard that graves were visible some years ago.[2] The present farm-house (Rowley) stands in the south-east corner of a small square entrenchment apparently, about 260 yards south-west of the camp, and seems to have been built out of the stones of the castle. Though Surtees mentions the entrenchment, it is probable he never saw it.[3] Had Hutchinson known of

---

[2] "There are the remains of other chapels, one at Old Hall, one at Rowley Gillet, &c., &c., but no evidence of their date or rights has come to our knowledge."—Hutchinson, vol. ii., p. 445.

[3] "There are some remains of a square entrenchment at Rowley, on the height of the hill above the Derness."—Surtees, vol. ii., p. 342.

it, he would perhaps have made something out of it, from the valuable deeds he saw relating to Esh, Cornsey, and Hedley ;[4] as it is, he does not seem to have mentioned it.

Though Rowley is now a part of Esh, or Ash, it is not certain that it belonged to the Manor originally, as would appear from an ancient map, where the part adjoining is marked as waste or common, otherwise the castellated building would probably appear to have been the ancient residence of the Ash family, before the present hall was built, which Surtees conjectures, from two shields of arms on the gateway of the court-yard, to have been built by Sir Edward Smythe, the first baronet, after 1660.[5] Thus, it is just possible it may have belonged to Cornesey, and even have been the dwelling of "Will-o'-the-Rawe, and Dionesia, his wife," in the fourteenth century.[6] Still, we find that "the family of De Esh had lands here (in Cornsey), and Allan de Esh, then the bishop's forester, took, by virtue of the grant of Walter, the son of Hugh de Middleton ;"[7] also, that in 1428, Johan (widow of Bland), conveyed to trustees several manors and vills, and also " 2 mess. cc. acress in cornehowe."[8] The family of De Esh likewise " possessed a city house in the Bailey, Durham, built against the castle wall ;" and further, "that the manors and vills of Esh, and Ushawe, the Hugh, and Underside (which comprise the manor, with the exception of Rowley), were held of the bishop, by military service of the value of twelve marks."[9] Hence it seems likely that the castle was the property and

---

[4] " By several conveyances in the fourteenth century, it appears that Cornsey, under the distinction of Cornsey-row, gave a local name to its possessor, among whom we find Will-o'-the-Raw, and Dionesia-o'-the-Raw."—Hutchinson, under Cornsey and Hedley, vol. iii., p. 387. On this passage Surtees runs thus : "In 1350, William del Rawe [*Cornsay Raw ?*] died, seised, jointly with Dionesia his wife, of half the manor of Cornsow." The query and brackets are the historian's, and seem to imply a doubt, that the name *Raw* was taken from the *Row*, but as we imagine from the *Camp.*—Surtees, vol. ii., p. 340.

[5] Edward Smythe, of Esh, Esq., was created a baronet the 28th February, 1660.

[6] Hutchinson, vol. iii., p. 387.

[7] *Idem.*

[8] *Idem*, p. 467.

[9] At this period of our uncertainty, Mr. Raine, of Durham, the learned historian of North Durham, &c., directed our attention to a note in Surtees's " Hist. Durham," vol. ii., p. 340, which seems to affix the name *Chestres* to the spot called Rowley Castle, and thus to strengthen our supposition of its Roman origin. Subsequently, Mr. Raine was so kind as to examine the Almoner's book. He says, " I enclose for you the Charter from the Almoner's book, transcribed and translated according to your request. The point is,

I think, fairly established, that you have found a new Roman camp."

" LIBER ELEMOSINARII.

" *Mickleton*, No. 28.

" Omnibus videntibus vel audientibus has litteras Hugo, filius Roberti de Midelton salutem.—Noverit universitas vestra me concessisse dedisse et hac presenti carta mea confirmasse Deo et Sancto Cutberto et Monachis Dunelmensibus et eorum Elemosinariæ viginti acras terræ arabilis in villa de Corneshou cum tofto et crofto et duabus acris quas Willielmus Pollard tenuit in eadem villa, scilicet novem acras et unam rodam in Raggepeth versus orientem, et decem acras et tres rodas in Whonm̄e ad Pilebrom et ad Baldwineshened et unam acram juxta viam Episcopi a villa de Corneshou versus occidentem et tres rodas juxta Chestres versus orientem et unam rodam juxta Helfinespot et unam acram in predicto crofto tenendas et habendas de me et heredibus meis in liberam et puram et perpetuam elemosinam libere et quiete et solute ab servicio consuetudine exactione et demanda sicut aliqua elemosina liberius quiecius habetur vel possidetur cum omnibus aysiamentis liberis consuetudinibus libertatibus rectitudinibus et pertinenciis ad dictam villam de Corneshou et dictam terram pertinentibus. Ego autem et heredes mei dictam elemosinam dictis

place of defence of De Esh, against the inroads of the Scots and other northerns, along the Roman Watling Street, which at that early period, perhaps, had not been destroyed ; and that subsequently his successors removed to a more eligible situation, where the hall now stands. In proof of the antiquity of the inclosure of Rowley, it is stated that the fences belong to it all round, with the exception of Rowley Gelet.

The original approach to the camp would appear to have been along an old line of straight road, which on the south side of the brook seems to have been met by a traverse, with a way up on each side, leading to the west side of the camp. This old road joins the Watling Street at the nearest point, distant about half a mile. A more modern road approaches from the westward, near the present cart-road. After the Watling Street has crossed the Ash-road, it becomes more visible, and runs in a considerable ridge across some fields, on the east of Willshill, and along the road towards Lanchester, till we come to the turn off to Hamstiels, where some doubt may be expressed how it proceeds to the station. This doubt arises from the publication of a map by Hutchinson, in which the Watling Street is shown on the west of the station;[1] otherwise, it is clear enough, that making a slight bend to the east, at Square House, it was found in draining the land in a field on Hollin farm, is still faintly visible in crossing the road to Lanchester, and has been ploughed out in the fields of Greenwell,[2] some of the stones being still visible, and thus must have reached the river Browney at the precipitous scar, about 240 yards to the west of the present ford.[3] Why this bend was made to the eastward, does not now appear ; but it must be observed, that the river has changed its course here, and now

monachis contra omnes homines warantizabimus omni exceptione remota vel excusatione. Hiis testibus Waltero de Kam, Stephano de Korneshou, Willielmo de Hedeleye, Rogero fratre ipsius, Stephano fratre Willielmi quondam prioris, Waltero de Selesbi, Willelmo de Acle et multis aliis."

To all seeing or hearing these letters, Hugh, son of Robert de Midelton, greeting.—Know all men that I have granted, given, and by this my present charter confirmed to God and Saint Cuthbert, and to the Monks of Durham and their Almonery, twenty acres of arable land in the vill of Corneshou with a toft and croft, and two acres which William Pollard held in the same vill, to wit, nine acres and one rood in Raggepeth towards the east, and ten acres and three roods in Whonme at Pilebrom and at Baldewineshened, and one acre near the Bishop's way from the vill of Korneshou to the west, and three roods near Chestres towards the east, and one rood near Helfinespot, and one acre in the aforesaid croft, to have and to hold of me and my heirs in free, pure and perpetual alms, freely and peaceably, and released from service, custom, exaction and demand, as any other alms are more freely and peaceably held or possessed, together with all easements, free customs, liberties, rights and appurtenances to the said vill of Corneshou and to the said land belonging. I therefore and my heirs will warrant the said alms to the said Monks against all men, every exception or excuse being laid aside. These being witnesses, Walter de Kam, Stephan de Korneshou, William de Hedeleye, Roger his brother, Stephan brother of William formerly prior, Walter de Selesbi, William de Acle, and many others.

[1] History of Durham, vol. ii., p. 452.

[2] "The tenement called Greenwell (where the family resided before Ford was built) lies to the south across the water of Browney."—Surtees, p. 317.

[3] Near this spot, a stone, with a recumbent figure cut on it, perhaps a local deity of the stream, apparently Roman, was discovered, and is, with several others found at the station, in the care of Mr. Nicholas Greenwell.

offers obstacles where once it offered facilities for crossing perhaps, and there was a more gradual descent than would have been found further to the westward. Here, however, another bend must have taken place; and though tradition and the ploughman are all we have to depend on, it seems probable that, combined with a view of the general line, and the next known point immediately north of Margery Flat and the Newbiggin road, the Watling Street ran within about 75 yards of the wall of the station on the east. For the name of the station we can only refer to the several authors who have written on the subject, the majority of whom consider it to have been the *Epiacum* of Ptolemy, and the *Longovicum* of the Notitia.[4] (See Map-Sheet, No. 4.)

There seems little doubt that so large, sheltered, and fertile a valley as Lanchester would be inhabited by a pastoral people at an early age, and the British name, as usual, be found incorporated with the subsequent ones. The situation altogether resembles that of Compton, near Illsley, in Berkshire, particularly. if it be admitted that a British camp, like Perborough, once stood where the Roman station now does. It is 10 miles 1 furlong from Binchester, in a straight line, and 12 miles 3 furlongs by the Watling Street. The situation of the station is on an elevated tongue of land, between the river Browney and a small feeder of the Smallhope Beck. It is about half a mile to the west of Lanchester, about 200 feet above it, about 300 feet below the surrounding hills, and about 575 feet above the sea. The form of the work is a right-angled parallelogram, with the north and south fronts each 188 yards in length, and the east and west fronts 156 yards each, containing within the walls about six acres. Writers assert that there was a gateway in the centre of each front.[5] This is evidently the case now in the east and west fronts, but the two others are so obscured by rubbish, that it is not easy to say where the entrances were, though from faint traces of a communication each way through the centre of the work, it seems probable that the gateways were in the centre of each front. There is a circle of ground about the centre, slightly elevated, which is probably the foundations of some buildings; and towards the northern front a much more raised part, containing two compartments, each terminating in a circular part towards the west.

[4] This part of the subject received great attention from Mr. Hodgson the historian, and at one time the resident clergyman. He says, "Camden supposed Lanchester to be the *Longovicum* of the Notitia Imperii. His opinion was followed till Horsley endeavoured to prove that *Longovicum* was the Roman name of Lancaster, and that the tenth iter commenced at Lanchester. When the subject has met with due consideration, Camden's conjecture, we doubt not, will be preferred." "*Glanoventa* was not here; *Longovicum* and *Lineojugla* (of the anonymous Ravenna) I consider as the same; and as Ptolemy wrote his geography before the Romans had much destroyed the names of the British villages, this place might be called *Epiacum* in Hadrian's time, but in the reign of Theodosius the younger, have got the Latin name of *Longovicum;* and in the barbarous age of the corographia, be termed *Lineojugla.*" (Longovicum, a vision.) Admitting this, it is possible that the original British name *Cwm* may have become, from the task-work on the *road* the people had to perform in it, distinguished as *y-via-cum;* and when the fortress was built and enclosed, be known as *Llan-y-via-cum:* for it is conjectured that though the Latin language was never spoken by the natives, still *Via* must have been familiar to them.

[5] "There have been entrances in the middle of each side."—Surtees, vol. ii., p. 303.

The lower part of these compartments, when first opened, had small rude pillars of about two feet in height, supporting the floor of an upper room, the walls of which were painted in fresco apparently, a part of which may even now be seen. This is supposed to have been a bath, or perhaps the interior of a private residence, warmed with hot air from beneath.— (A hypocaust). The south-west angle appears not only rounded like the rest, as usual, but has foundations of a building on the inside, scarcely sufficient to have supported a tower, but like a barrack or residence with small compartments. The walls have been nearly destroyed, and all the ashlar work taken away, so that only the interior of the walls remains, and but a part only of that exists.[6] The interior is in pasture, and no doubt covers a rich mine of antiquities. The walls seem to have been surrounded by a ditch of about sixty feet in width, though now completely levelled, and on the west side there are slight indications of a double-ditch,[7] which possibly there may have been on the weakest side; for on each side but this, the natural fall of the ground is considerable, here it is nearly level; hence an extra ditch might have been necessary. The shape of the ground would offer accommodation for a much larger force than the station would contain; and, from faint traces of intrenchment on the south and west sides, it seems probable the spot was more extensively entrenched, and for a larger force at one time, to which the present enclosure would form but the prætorium.

On an examination of the map of the aqueducts said to have been traced from Woodlands, on the north side of Umber Hill, and by Colpike, on the south of it, and also the supposed junction at the entrance to Upper Houses, having at the same time spoken to old residents, we can offer no vestiges of this watercourse as at present existing within half a mile of the station, or the reservoir to which it led.[8] There seems to be an abundance of water on the hill in every direction, and in the south-east angle a drain from which the superfluous quantity would flow off. This sewer, formed of cut stone arched over, has been examined, running towards the centre, diminishing in size in that direction.[9]

Much has been written respecting Roman ways diverging from this position, but as we have expressed a doubt about the true entrance and exit of Watling Street, it will not be expected that the course of the lateral roads can be pointed out. There can be no doubt that roads diverged, one

---

[6] " The vallum has been probably near twelve feet in height. The outside is perpendicular, built of ashlar work in regular courses, the stones being about nine inches deep and twelve long; the interior is also of ashlar work, formed of thin stones laid tier above tier, slanting and covering each other featherwise, and run with mortar mixed with rough gravel. The thickness of the vallum, at the present surface, is eight feet, but diminishes gradually by parallel steps to about four feet at the summit. It has a double fosse on the west, and on the other sides the advantage of the sloping hill. The angles of the walls appear to have been guarded by round towers, and, like every Roman camp, there have been entrances in the middle of each side." (Surtees, vol. ii., p. 303.) The wall at present is most continuous and high on the south, in some places as much as nine feet.

[7] It is probable that these traces of ditches have been taken for the ruins of Watling Street.

[8] See Hodgson in Archæologia Æliana, vol. i., p. 121. In this examination we had the valuable assistance and experience of Mr. Nicholas Greenwell, of Lanchester.

[9] Verbal account from Mr. F. Greenwell, who examined it.

to the westward perhaps, and one along the present line of road towards Chester-le-Street. Another probably passed to the north-east by Maiden Law. But though these are evidently old lines of road, there are no remains now at Lanchester to lead to their discovery as Roman remains. The tumulus which it is presumed gave name to Maiden Law, has been removed; there is a paved road branching off about 280 yards towards Lanchester, in a north-west direction, called the Scots Road. It is probable it was used by that people in their way to Durham formerly. On the supposed Roman line towards Newcastle, and also on that towards Chester-le-Street, the name *Peth* occurs, which may be taken as evidence of great antiquity, Urpeth (Here-peth?), and Peth House.[1] The doubtful part of the Watling Street lies on each side the Lanchester station, from the Browney river, to the road between Lanchester and Newbiggin, which it is evident it crossed a little above the entrance to Margery Flat House, along the west edge of a triangular small field, called "*The Acre.*"

Both Brown and Robinson, the successive farmers of Margery Flat, assert, that in ploughing the long field, on the south of the brook, they found a more stony part on the east side than in any other part; should this have been the Roman way, it would have led to the centre of the station. Robinson found a number of shoes in the bog at the stream below, and one in particular with the foot in it and bound with a sandal leather strap.[2] Bones were also found in this boggy part, which before it was drained was about four feet deep. If what these men describe as a stony part was the road, it would have cut this bog, in which they found no traces, though abundance of shoes. Hence, it is presumed, that the road, keeping our assumed line, would cross a little below this boggy place, and perhaps becoming a dam have contributed to form the bog. From the above-mentioned field called "The Acre," our road is visible enough, as it bends gently round a natural contour of the hill, and descends to the low ground between the Lizards and low meadows. Watling Street is clearly discernible about 200 yards to the west of the small farm-house called Lizards, and faint traces of it may be seen till we come to the turnpike road, which it crossed about 350 yards on the west of Esp Green Farm-house. On the east of our road at this place, and about 175 yards south of the turnpike road, are the foundations of a chapel, probably one of ease to Lanchester, before the village of Leadgate was built.[3] Crossing the road, Watling Street appears to bend a little to the westward, and to run about thirty yards in front of both Low and High Woodside houses, perhaps to avoid a slight fall in the ground to the east of the latter house, but the traces here are exceedingly obscure, and though supported by local authority, we are not prepared to deny that the straight line was not preserved, which would have brought the way out at the same point, the meeting of the three roads at the west end of Iveston.

---

[1] Hodgson in Arch. Æliana.

[2] This shoe, with the bones still in it, and a part of the leather strap, is in the possession of Mr. F. Greenwell, at Durham.

[3] "There are the remains of other chapels; one at Old Hall, one at Rowley Gillet, one at Collierly, and another at Esp Green."—Hutchinson's Hist. Dur., vol. ii., p. 445.

From the cross road at Iveston the Watling Street runs straight towards the village of Leadgate, though the present road is not precisely in the middle of it, but first seems a little to the eastward, and at Leadgate Farm, so far to the eastward of it, that the remains have been ploughed out, and some still exist, close to the wall of the road and stack-yard. About 130 yards north of the farm-house, we attain the highest ground : here, the road appears to have made a slight bend to the eastward and to have gone straight to the next higher ground, about nine furlongs, where it attains the height of about 840 feet above the sea. This spot is called Bunker's Hill.[4] In passing the village of Leadgate we lose the traces of the line, but should suppose the road to have gone a little on the west of the turnpike gate-house at the cross roads. At Bunker's Hill the road is still visible, though the stones have been taken off, or broken up for the present road, with which it seems to coincide, and continues to be identical with it, as we conceive, to Ebchester,[5] but on this we shall have to offer some opposite evidence. Dr. Hunter relates,[6] that the foundation of a watch-tower was visible in his day, " about a Roman mile and half south of Ebchester ; " we have sought unsuccessfully for these remains.

When we arrive within about 400 yards of Ebchester, the road makes a considerable bend to the eastward, to descend the declivity and pass the brook diagonally to advantage ; and though there are no remains of the Watling Street to be seen, there can be little doubt that this has been the line. The situation of Ebchester, which is allowed to be the Vindomora[7] of the Itineraries, is remarkably good, not only in a picturesque, but in a military point of view. It stands on an eminence, between the river Derwent and a small brook, having the former on the north, and the latter on its west and south sides. Though the walls have been taken down, and even the foundations excavated for the materials, the rampart is sufficiently discernible to ascertain the original form of the work, which seems to have been a square of about four acres in extent, with the church-yard in the south-west angle. It is probable that there were two gates through which the present road runs from Shotley Bridge to Newcastle, but no signs of them are now apparent. From faint traces of a ditch running to the westward, in prolongation of the north and south front, it is probable there was at one time an outwork on that side, as a *procestrium*, advancing to the edge of the declivity over the brook, where the present road, which we take to be the Watling Street, reaches to.

---

[4] In the field between the road and the farm-house are traces of some entrenchments, but not sufficiently connected to make any certainty out respecting them.

[5] " Ebchester is upon the river Derwent, and on that account has a strong claim to the appellation Derventio."—Hodgson in Longovicum.

[6] Surtees, Hist. Durham, vol. ii., p. 300.

[7] " This, therefore, is no doubt *Vindomora*."—Horsley, Brit. Romana. " The little chapel of Ebchester, a farmhold, and a few thatched cottages, stand within the very area of the ancient *Vindomora*, if Vindomora it be, for the point is by no means stated as beyond controversy." —Surtees, Hist. Durham. This name is probably derived from '*wynn—white*, or *fair*, and *dwfr—water*, in reference to the river Derwent (Dwfr-wynn), with a Latin termination, perhaps ; for *fawr—great*, would not apply to the relative size of the camp ; nor *morfa—near the sea*, to its position in the country.

From this cross road it is presumed that the Roman Way continued down to the river on the east side of the brook, in the line of the present road, and we can only account for the narrowness of it now by the brook having washed away a part of it in the course of centuries; it is right to state, however, that no signs of the ancient road are visible except the suitableness of the line.[8]   (See Map-Sheet, No. 4.)

We were accompanied, in our examination, by the Rev. Mr. Stubbs, and two other of the oldest inhabitants, Mr. Cuthbert Surtees,[9] and Mr. George Rutherford; we examined a way up a brook, 440 yards to the westward, called Bludderburn Dean, traditionally said to be the course of Watling Street, but we saw no sufficient traces to suppose it to be the line, and think it too far off to afford that mutual protection which in other cases seems to have been attained between the stations and the road.[1]   Though the station was small in extent, it will be seen, on a survey of the position, that an advantageous and defensible area of 20 acres might have been taken up, and from some faint traces of occupation, it is probable was at one time adopted.   Ebchester is about 6 miles 3 furlongs from Lanchester, in a straight line, and 6 miles 4 furlongs by the Watling Street; 300 feet above the sea, and 100 feet above the river.   Crossing the Derwent, we enter Northumberland on the Derwentwater property, and have to acknowledge, with thanks, the great assistance we received from Mr. Grey, of Dilston, and, through him, of Mr. John Fewster, the tenant who holds the land through which the Watling Street ran on Newlands Farm.   Where it crossed the river, Derwent appears as little known on the north side as on the south.   We reach *an ascent* about 400 yards from the stream, where there are now faint traces of a stony ridge, and Mr. Fewster, and his father before him, have constantly laboured to clear the place for cultivation. This is the spot where the traditional line before mentioned branches off to Bludderburn Dean, and Mr. John Fewster says, that "Mr. Cuthbert Surtees, of Newcastle" (who originally lived at Ebchester) "states, that an altar was found about 60 years ago which was in the possession of Mr. John Surtees, late of Ebchester, and presented to the late Henry Swinburne, Esq., of Hamsterley Hall, near Ebchester.   He states, that the above was found close adjoining the Derwent, near the west side of West Haugh," (opposite Bludderburn Dean), "in Newlands Haugh Farm."   "It appears that the altar was about 3 feet high, and about 16 inches in diameter, with a cup upon it and an illegible inscription below."[2]

[8] We could neither see nor hear anything of the piers of a bridge, mentioned by Hutchinson, "supposed by some to be part of a Roman bridge," nor trace the aqueduct said by Dr. Hunter to have "brought water to the baths;" that which seems like one appears more modern, and is said to have conveyed water to a brewery.

[9] His father had been agent to the Derwentwater property, in this particular neighbourhood.

[1] "At the distance of a Roman mile and a half to the south (according to Hunter), the foundation of a square watch tower was discovered, about six or eight yards west of the military way."—Surtees' Durham, vol. ii., p. 301.   We have inquired and looked about for this watch tower, and can only see a faint trace of a ditch 660 yards south of the cross from Medomsley to Shotley Bridge, and a circular hole near a pond 264 yards north of the same cross road, which could by any possibility be taken for ancient remains; therefore we suppose the plough has obliterated all signs referred to.

[2] There is a small altar dedicated to

We notice the authority for this altar, because some may suppose the occurrence of it so close to the traditional line may be some confirmation of the truth of the supposition.[3] From *the ascent* above-mentioned, the road makes a bend towards Whittonstall, and ran straight, apparently, to a slight increase in the ascent about 1500 yards forward, and thence, by a very gentle bend to the westward, straight into Whittonstall. It is visible where it crosses the present road and enters the wood called East Woody Pasture, at the west corner of the field called Holywell Field; the blacksmith at Newlands points it out crossing his fields, about 100 yards to the east of the forge, joining the present road at the turn off to Headley Mill. At Whittonstall, the present road and Watling Street are presumed to be the same through the village; and at the north end both make a bend to the eastward, to ease the descent; indeed, the pavement is still visible all the way up, at intervals, as well as in the village. At Whittonstall are the remains of a trench and rampart which surrounded the ancient residence called, as we are informed by Mr. Grey, Whittingstall, alias Quittingstall, in a deed dated 27th October, 1623. These remains are on the highest part of the hill, and about 200 yards from Watling Street; the spot was recently called the Hall. The road at Whittonstall attains the height of 720 feet above the sea.[4]

About a mile—instead of half a mile, as stated by Horsley—from Whittonstall, " is a remarkable turn " in the Watling Street; " and at this turn," on the west side, at the distance of about 30 yards from the road, " is an exploratory fort of above 30 yards square, the situation of it is high, and the prospect very large " towards the north; "and near it is a tumulus, which I found to consist mostly of stones covered with green turf."[5] This tumulus has been removed it is supposed, as no account can be heard of it; but the fort is still traceable, though, since the enclosure of the common, the plough has nearly obliterated it. The spot is called Castle Hill. The Way, which from Whittonstall to this fort had run straight, changes its bearing considerably, and apparently takes lower ground unnecessarily to rise again, but an examination of the brook in advance will show that a precipitous part of the bank would have offered very considerable difficulties in a straight line. In crossing the Stockfield brook the present road appears to be about 30 yards below the Watling Street, which seems to run straight from the fort, to the high ground

Mars, and a small centurial stone, built into the wall at the Parsonage House; and another inscribed stone built into a carthouse adjoining the churchyard. We have pointed these out to Mr. Bruce, who no doubt will make out the nearly illegible inscriptions on each. It is probable that these are figured in Hutchinson.

[3] Had Watling Street passed down Bludderburn Dean, it would have been seen probably in the fields immediately on the south as it descended the hill; but, on inquiry from Mr. John Bradden, of West Law, who held that particular land called East Law Farm; he never saw the remains of any road down that way, and he has always considered the Watling Street to go the line of the present road. No traces were seen of that remarkable construction of the road near Ebchester, " formed in three distinct parts, with four ditches, a centre road, with a narrow road on each side for foot-passengers, twelve feet wide."—Hutchinson, vol. ii., p. 549. Oct. ed.

[4] We are desirous to acknowledge, with thanks, the assistance we received at Whittonstall from the Rev. Mr. Marshall.

[5] Horsley's Brit. Romana.

between the two brooks, and thence with a fresh bearing to the turn off to Hindley Farm, where a part of it may still be seen in the present road. At this turn off the Watling Street takes a new direction, bearing a little more north; and at the next small brook the present road is wholly on the west of the line; and at about 110 yards in advance it leaves the Watling Street, which continues the straight line across the fields, as pointed out by Mr. Angus of Broomley, and some old residents on the spot. This part of the line passed about 260 yards south-west of Broomley Farm house at its nearest point, and may be seen as a ridge crossing the road from Broomley to Shotley about 150 yards from the turn off. The line of bearing, where the Watling Street joins the road at the turn off to Raw House, is continued along the present road to the town, and straight forward down Whiteside Wood, where traces are still to be seen, into an angle of the turnpike-road, about 250 yards above the turnpike-gate. Between this and the gate the road seems to cross our line, which apparently made a slight curve into the valley to pass the brook, running probably on the west of the turnpike-house, under the school, and close to the small foot-bridge, if not over it, skirting the building on the west of the Riding Mills, and by a similar curve regains its line at the horse-trough, where the turnpike-road crosses it again; and some traces of it may be seen in the meadow, north of the mill, opposite the road leading to the Riding Mill Station on the Newcastle and Carlisle Railway. Its course thence, at the back of the buildings of Riding House on the east of the present road, was pointed out by Thomas March, who has long worked on the farm, and has heard from old people the quantity of stones removed from the line. It runs straight to the turnpike-house at Farnley; and about four furlongs before it reaches that place, its line may be traced across a small rill, where the ground on each side of it is damp and discoloured, as if the deep-lying drain of the road still performed its office, after a lapse of so many centuries: near this, we saw it cut by a trench to drain the fields, imperfect, but distinguishable. It is necessary to be thus particular, as Armstrong has carried it in his map further to the westward.

It will be seen from this that the road makes a slight curve to the westward to cross the Riding Mill Brook, or Dipton Burn, and does not assume its straight course till it has been crossed for some distance by the present road. The most remarkable instance of this practice we have ever seen is in the Fosse-way between Bath and Cirencester, where it is repeatedly done, and always up the stream. Our line joins the turnpike-road about 330 yards before we reach the gate. At Farnley turnpike-gate there is no trace of the Watling Street; but about 90 yards on the south of it, in the angle formed by the turnpike-road and the lane running south-west as the boundary between the Riding and Corbridge, is a tumulus, having much the appearance of being artificial, placed at a bend in the Watling Street, and commanding a view of Corbridge. About 50 yards on the south of Farnley Farm house the Watling Street again appears, branching off as it were from the turnpike-road. Traces of it may be seen in the field opposite the house, where the tenant describes the quantity of stones he has taken out of it. It continues its course at about 100 yards from the turnpike-road, on the south of it, till we arrive at Tinkler Bank, where it is about 175 yards to the south; and at about 330 yards beyond the turn down the declivity to Corbridge, the Watling Street crossed the turnpike-road diagonally, and in a graceful curve descended the only easy declivity along the precipitous bank of the river Tyne. It seems to have crossed the turnpike-road from Corbridge to Hexham, where a road leaves it to Dilston Hall, and is there lost in the alluvial soil; but between Farnley and this last point the course was pointed out satisfactorily by the tenant, who has observed it in cultivating the fields, and by the person who drained the land. (Messrs. Joseph Lee and Thomas Harle.)

About half a mile above Corbridge Bridge are some remains of an ancient bridge on the south bank,[6] and to these remains the course of the road seems to tend, but no traces whatever can now be seen of it. Landing on the opposite bank, we ascend about 100 feet to the site of Colcester, the *Corstopitum* of the Itineraries,[7] the centre of which is about 665 yards north-west by west of Corbridge Church tower. Desirous to notice such Roman roads as fall in along the line of Watling Street, it will be expected we should notice that which is usually represented as joining our road here from the south-west, and called occasionally the *Maiden Way*. And here we take Thomas Harle again as our guide, whose experience in draining the land was found useful. From the ruins of the bridge it would seem to have gone in the direction of Dilston Hall, passing about 40 yards on the east of the turnpike-gate, some faint traces being ploughed up just before crossing the road; thence to cross the Devil's-water at Dilston Mill, where we find a pier of an ancient bridge still standing; thence under the lodge, and about 60 yards on the south of the house called Park South Farm; and thence by a bend towards the wood. Horsley observes :—" The place where the station has been is called Corbow, and Colcester; and according to the account I had when I was there, Corbow is a small place included in Colcester, which contains several acres." "It is probable that the former has been the station, or perhaps the prætorium only, and the latter both station and town. I am much of opinion that the names have been Corcester and Corburgh." (Brit. Romana.) (See Map-Sheet, No. 4.)

Dr. Todd (in Phil. Trans., No. 330), supposes the name Colcester to have been Herculcester. The same learned doctor also observes that Corbridge was called, in the charter of Henry I., Colbrige, and Colburgh; but I rather incline to think that Corburgh has been the name next to the Roman Corstopitum."[8]—(Brit. Romana). This opinion may be strengthened

---

[6] These remains are clearly to be seen at low and clear water in summer; they consist of large dressed stones laid in the bed of the river, and bolted together with iron and lead cramps. Viewed from the south bank at present, the bridge would seem to have crossed the river obliquely; but we are inclined to think that when the bridge was made, the current of the river was not what it is now exactly, but has been such as to have coincided nearly with a line at right angles to the course of the bridge.

[7] " Whoever views the adjoining heap of ruins called *Colcester* will pronounce it a Roman station."—Camden's Brit., p. 493. " The place where the station has been is called *Corbow* and *Colcester*".—Horsley, Brit. Romana. The spot is called *Colcester* in an old map of the Commons enclosure, A.D. 1776.

[8] *Col* is an *eminence*, and would apply equally well with *Cor*.

by the form of the ancient place, as traced out from the foundations still remaining and those displaced, clearly pointed out by the tenant and the drainer of the fields. The form is an irregular ellipse, with a transverse diameter of about 420 and a conjugate of 280 yards; the former bearing 60°, and the latter about 30° from the northern course of the Watling Street; leading to the supposition that the Romans found a work of defence here,[9] and connected it with their great road. This would probably be called *caer*, a *camp*, by the British; the corruption to *cor*, and subsequently pronounced *col*, will not surprise those who have observed the peculiar effect produced by the letter *r*, in the delivery of a native Northumbrian: the name *Corbow* is no longer to be heard of. The situation is such as either the British or Romans would have chosen; a precipitous bank to the river on one side, and a gentle fall in every other direction. The area may have been about twenty-two acres. It is 9 miles 3 furlongs from Ebchester, in a straight line, and 10 miles by the Watling Street.

At Minsteracres, which is about 6 miles south of Corbridge, and 3 west of Whittonstall, are four altars which originally came from Corbridge. They are about 3 feet 6 inches in height; one of them is formed of three headless figures representing the Deæ Matres, and has been figured, as well as the other three, we believe, in Horsley's Britannia Romana.

At Colcester the Watling Street is easily discernible, on the north running in a straight line for Stagshaw Bank, bearing N. by E. Its course is along a field lane for a short distance, and is there readily traced to within sixty yards of the brook, called by some writers "Col," and by others "Cor," but now Corbridge Burn. About 100 yards north of the brook it appears very perfect, and so continues to where the Sandoe Road joins the turnpike road; here the western fence of the turnpike road stands on the east side of the Watling Street, and as they run together the former crosses the latter diagonally, so that at the S.E. corner of Stagshaw Close grounds, where the road turns off to Hexham, the west fence of the turnpike road is on the middle of the Roman way. At this spot the turnpike road turns a little to the eastward to ease the ascent, so that the whole of the Watling Street seems to be within the grounds of Stagshaw Close.[1] As the road gradually returns to the westward it crosses the Watling Street, so that about the lodge both may be considered in one, and so they continue to the stinted pasture called Stagshaw Bank. At this spot the Watling Street makes a bend of 2° to the westward, for about 900 yards, and about the middle of this line is a small declivity to a brook, which divides Stagshaw Bank from the township of Portgate.[2] On this declivity, on the west side the road, is a quadrangular earthwork, having the

---

[9] Had there been no British place of defence here, it does not seem probable that the Watling Street would have come so far to the westward; but having gained the level of the Tyne at Riding Mill, the rise to Farnley would have been avoided, the river would have been crossed near the tunnel in the railway, and the height to Stagshaw Bank have been gained diagonally, rather than as in the present manner, and without the nearly right angle which it makes at Corbridge.

[1] In this part of the line we were kindly assisted by Mr. Crawhall, the proprietor.

[2] Perhaps this *declivity* has given the name to Stagshaw *Bank*.

appearance of an exploratory fort, nearly rectangular, containing about 1¼ acre, and with two entrances apparently, one on the east, and the other on the north; but the whole is so indistinct that its intention as a place of defence might be questioned. It is probable that this is the camp written "*Roman Fort*" in Warburton's Map, but it is placed there a furlong to the south of the small stream. It must be observed, however, that its position would give, at an equal distance of ¼ of a mile each way, a commanding view of the road both to the north and south, and its situation on the bank of the stream would offer a defence towards the north, supposing it to have been a post connected with Colcester before the works at the wall were constructed. The road makes a further bend easterly of about 20°, at 180 yards before it arrives at the Roman wall, and runs straight from that angle to Bewclay Bank, a distance of ten furlongs.

It may be proper to notice here, that the township of Portgate extends a considerable distance on each side of the meeting of Watling Street with the Roman Wall; and it seems possible, that the name originally applied to the cross-road, as *Port*, an *entrance*, and *Gate*, the *northern* word for a *way* or *road;* for it is presumed that the buildings now called Portgate, are much subsequent to the naming of the township. Warburton seems to have taken these signs of ancient occupation for a Roman town, and would fix *Gallana* about here, and the crossing of the Devil's Causeway.[3]

At Portgate the Roman wall crosses the Watling Street, the turnpike-road being on the wall, and its ditch on the north of the road. The Roman ditch and rampart are parallel to the wall at this place, and about 80 yards on the south side of it. It does not appear, however, that any road branched off from this part of the Roman wall so as to connect with the Devil's Causeway, though it is possible there may have been one from Halton Chesters through Great Wittington.[4] It seems probable that Armstrong, in his map, has hit on the true junction of the Devil's Causeway with Watling Street, at Bewclay, where our road makes a fresh turn of 25° more to the westward, and runs straight towards Colwell and Little Swinburne. The ground at Bewclay is elevated, and, being at a turn in the road, would serve well for an exploratory fort, not

[3] "Having discovered a very entire military way (vulgarly called the Devil's Causeway) twenty-two feet broad, and paved with stone, to range through this country from north to south, and at Thornton near the river Wansbeck, *Portgate on the Roman wall,* and Oldtown in Allendale (all standing thereon)—visible remains of Roman garrisons,—I hope none of our modern antiquaries will be displeased at my entitling them *Glanoventa, Gallana, Alone,* since a multitude of reasons may be offered to increase the probability of it beyond any places yet made choice of."—Note on Warburton's Map in the Brit. Mus.

[4] Richard of Cirencester's Fourth Iter.

"without noticing either Ebchester or Corbridge," passes "over the Tyne to Halton Chester-on-the-Wall. Here separating from the north Watling Street, it ran with the Ermyn Street, now known in Northumberland by the name of the Devil's Causeway, to the bank of the Coquet and the Tweed."—Note to the Fourth Iter. in Bohn's Edit., p. 486. Horsley mentions a Castellum at the junction of Watling Street, and another about a furlong to the east; but the traces of these can with difficulty be made out now, the wear at the cross road and along the whole line has obliterated much that was clear in his day.

only for the Watling Street, but also for the supposed branch called the Devil's Causeway.   It would be in sight of Moat Law and Grindstone Law, both exploratory camps overlooking the line of the Devil's Causeway, and thus keep up a communication between the two lines; it does not come out satisfactorily, however, that any remains can be confidently traced as works of defence, though the rough ground immediately on the north of the buildings looks very like entrenched remains.   The present road to the farm was not the ancient branch, it is conjectured, but one now closed up by the side of the wall, just where the turn in Watling Street is made; if this be the Devil's Causeway, it has more the appearance of a British than a Roman way.  ·Of this spot General Roy observes, "At Bewclay, about two miles north from Portgate, in Northumberland, a branch, called the Devil's Causeway, goes off the Watling Street to the right, keeping between it and the sea." (Milit. Antiq., p. 103.)

Descending the hill, we arrive at Erring Bridge, the stream at which is said by some writers to be the Dennisbourne of Bede[5] and Hallington, the Heaven-field where the Christian Oswald overthrew the forces of the Pagan Penda in 635.[6]   North-east from this bridge, at a distance of about $3\frac{1}{2}$ miles, is a remarkable hill, called Moat Law, with an entrenchment on it of about $1\frac{1}{2}$ acre, surrounding a tumulus, which seems to have been used as a fire-beacon;[7] which, as it commands an extensive view on all sides, and also a considerable extent of the Roman wall, seems probable enough.   Its height is about 850 feet above the sea; and those who believe in the existence of temples to the worship of the sun, may here find a suitable position.   Between this height and the road, about a mile east of Bingfield, is another small entrenchment on a hill called Grinstone Law; the north-east part has been destroyed in quarrying for stone, and the whole thing is very obscure, but it seems to have been nearly square, about two acres, with an entrance on the west side, which was defended by a tumulus.   There are two ditches, diverging from each other, on Duns Moor, which seem more natural than artificial.   At about two miles from Erring Bridge we reach Swinbourne and Colwell, where, in ancient times, the recesses of the whinstone rocks must have afforded ample shelter to the opposing forces of an invading army, and an examination of the ground will show that it was a formidable pass.

On the west side the wood is Bird's Law, where a skeleton was discovered some years since in opening a quarry: it had a sword by its side, which had fallen to decay; but two copper vessels were in good preservation, one of which is now in the possession of John Elliot, living near the spot; it is in shape like a small basin, of about four inches in diameter. Swinburne Castle is a modern house, built by the ancestors of the present owner, Mr. Riddle, out of the ruins of the old castle, which perhaps occupied the place of a more ancient work : it is built on the precipitous bank of the Swinburne, just after it has found a passage through the

---

[5] Bede, Ecc. His., Book 3, chap. i. and ii. (Bohn's Ed., p. 110.)

[6] "Dr. Smith (App. to Bede, p. 730) says, that about a mile beyond Bingfield

to the north is Hallington, anciently Havenfelth or Heavenfield."—*Idem.*

[7] Additions in Gough's Camden, vol. iii., p. 510 ; from Wallis's Nat. His., p. 114.

whinstone rocks ;[8] the situation is very beautiful, and the form of the grounds most diversified. About 700 yards to the south of the mansion are several tumuli, and a remarkable upright stone, the height of which is 11 feet, the breadth 3 ft. 6 in., and thickness 1 ft. 6 in., tapering towards the top like an open hand. The largest of the tumuli was opened lately, to take the stones of which it is composed to repair a bridge ; in it were found five stone coffins, each about 4 feet long, and 2½ feet wide ; they contained bones and charcoal : each coffin was covered with a rough flat stone, and resting on the rock ; they were placed irregularly in the mound, which was originally about 50 yards long and 5 feet high.[9] These memorials may commemorate an engagement, to which the ground seems well adapted as a defensive position, having the steep banks of the Colwell brook on the left, and the precipitous edge of the Swinburne on the right, with the irregular defiles of the rocky ground in the rear.

Returning to the road, at about 250 yards from the lodge, we came to what may be considered as the gorge of the pass, for the rocks project so much on each side that advantage must have often been taken of their recesses in times of warfare. On the west is an eminence called Ox Hill, irregularly conical, the top of which seems to have been improved by art into a redoubt, with one entrance towards the Watling Street and within 90 yards of it; and between this rock and the Roman Catholic chapel are foundations of ancient buildings. At this spot the present turnpike bears to the eastward, leaving the remains of the Roman way plainly discernible to within 200 yards of the brook, when it turns to the west to ease the declivity to the ford over the Swinburne. Before descending to this ford, we must notice a still more perfect work of some ancient defenders of this pass ; it is on the top of one of the whinstone rocks called the Blue Crag, is about 800 yards north of Colwell, and 700 yards east of our road. Naturally it is an isolated mass of whinstone, of about an acre, in the form of a wedge, the back and sides offering natural defences, and the edge stoutly defended by a rampart of stones ; the upper part is divided from the lower by a continuation of this rampart of stones, and within this upper division are several circles of stones of about twenty-five or thirty feet in diameter, similar to what we have seen on Ingleborough in Yorkshire, and Carn Engley in Pembrokeshire, which are supposed to be British camps.[1] Immediately on the north of this camp is a smaller and less

---

[8] These rocks, which are presumed to be of igneous origin, would seem to have been poured out contemporaneously with the associated sedimentary strata ; but on examination they have a similar stratum of soft schistose rock, both above and below, from which the people select slate pencils, and which may be taken to be altered rock, heated by the mass injected between the strata along the line of least resistance. These beds of trap are frequently rudely columnar, yet dip to the south-east in conformity with the accompanying coal measures, as if elevated with them. At Swinburne Castle the outcrop is so low, and so overlaid by the super-incumbent beds, as nearly to disappear ; and at this spot, either through a fissure or fault, the brook has gained a passage ; this is a good place to observe the accompanying strata.

[9] Mr. Riddle, the proprietor, was so good as to allow his map of the grounds to be made use of, and to send his steward to point out the remains, from whom the above account was taken.

[1] "The houses of the Britons," says Henry, "were not like ours at present, or those of the Romans in those times, divided into several distinct apartments ; but consisted of one large circular room, or hall, with a fire in the middle, around

strong one, on Green Crag, having similar marks of occupation, though not so extensive or perfect; and on the east are other lines of occupation or dwellings.   Horsley's map shows an ancient road passing up from the Tyne in this direction through Colwell: it is probable there was always a way in this direction, but whether by the Five Lane Ends, or the castle, we are not certain.   An examination of these remains about Swinburne leads to the conclusion that it was well peopled in former times, and that many contests have taken place in its neighbourhood.   It does not appear that local history says much about it, except that in the reign of Edward I. Swinburne Castle was in the possession of Peter de Gunnerton, who held it of the barony of Bywell, by the service of two knights' fees of the old feoffment.[2]   (See Map-Sheet, No. 5.)

We shall see, however, that in the time of the Romans it was considered as a pass of some consequence; for, at a short distance from the brook, the line of way having assumed a new direction, falls into the former line where the present road joins it, though the traces in the fields are very obscure;   and at this place, both on the east and on the west, at the distance of about 550 yards, on similar hills, called Camp Hill, are two four-sided and nearly rectangular camps, about ¼ acre each, with two similar entrances on the east and west fronts.   They have been levelled so completely, that it is difficult to make out their forms precisely; but enough remains to lead to the presumption that they are of Roman construction; redoubts, or exploratory forts, placed in the most favourable position for taking in the rear any body of men attempting to dispute the passage of a force advancing to the northwards; and perhaps of supporting that small body which was possibly established on Oxhill, in the gorge of the pass.   One of these camps is on a farm called Little Swinburne; and the other on that called Rever Crag.   There are other camps which may be considered to form part of the defences of Swinburne Castle; at about a mile and a half on the west of the road, on a farm called Camp Hill, or Pity Me.   The most southerly of these is elliptical, the diameters of which are about 43 and 50 yards.   It had but one entrance apparently, opposite which, on the outside, is a ring of stones which probably had been a tumulus.   On the north of this, between the houses at Camp Hill, is another, conforming somewhat to the ground, and in the shape of an irregular pentagon, approaching in its mutilated form to a semicircle. The area is about an acre, and the entrance seems to have been on the south side.   On the south-west of this, in much lower ground, part on the farm of Rever Crag, and part on that of Camp Hill, is another, similar in form to that last mentioned, with an area of about the same extent.   Still further north than any of these, about 450 yards north of the North House at Camp Hill, is an entrenchment quite unlike any of the others, approaching a square in form, and containing about ¼ of an

which the whole family and visitants, men, women, and children, slept on the floor, in one continued bed of straw or rushes."—Mackenzie's Hist. View, vol. i., p. 5.
² " In the reign of Edward II. it was the seat and manor of Adam de Swinburn; it was afterwards in the knightly family of Widdrington for many generations; and subsequently in that of Riddell, in which it still remains."—Mackenzie's Hist. View, vol. ii., p. 221.

acre. Within the area are lines of division, and one circular compartment, as if it had been an entrenched residence rather than a regular camp. These camps are so placed on the high lands looking towards the west, that they seem as if they had been made by different people at different times, as a part of the defences of Swinburne Castle and Gunnerton.

Proceeding on our road, we arrive at Long Crag, where the line makes a new direction, a change of 4° more to the northward, and in about two miles further we come to Cowden, and Tone Inn. Possibly, these places may have derived their names from a small exploratory camp upon each. About 650 yards on the west of the road there is one of them in one of the detached plantations within the Cowden property. The name, Camp Hill, preserves the remembrance of the work, otherwise it is so ploughed down as to be nearly invisible; it is partly within the plantation, and partly without, that within being much the more perfect. It is nearly rectangular, and about the same size as the two last mentioned. The same remark will apply to the other on Tone, about 350 yards north-west of Tone Inn, which is in a similar plantation. About four furlongs beyond Tone Inn, the road makes another bend of about 13° more to the eastward. On the hill above Waterfalls Farm house, where once stood a cairn, is fixed a long cylindrical stone, like a Roman mile-stone, which was taken out of the side of the road, nearly opposite where it stands, when the road was lowered to improve the ascent; its height out of the ground 4 feet 9 inches, and its circumference 3 feet 9 inches. It is said to be 2 feet in the earth. No letters or marks were ever seen upon it. It is presumed to be the same mentioned by Hodgson,[3] and now marking the spot where " Lord Derwentwater assembled his adherents previous to his ill-fated expedition."—(Mackenzie's Hist. View, vol. ii. p. 334).

A short distance further brings us to Four Laws, where, opposite the 13th milestone from Corbridge, and 90 yards from the road, on the west side of it, is a Roman camp, rectangular, rectilinear, the angles rounded off, and with three gates, each with an inflexion of the rampart for its defence, but now no visible traverse in front. The ditch also is very imperfectly seen on three of the sides, but clearly distinguishable on the west, on which side there appears to have been no gateway. The sides of this camp are 174 yards, forming a square of about six acres. The gateway next the road is nearly in the centre of the front, but both the others are only about one-third the length of the front, from the east, which has been said to be the proper proportion, presuming the east to be the Decuman Gate. (Gen. Roy's Milit. Antiq.) This camp does not appear to have been mentioned by historians;[4] it may have been a summer camp to Risingham, from which it is not more than 19 furlongs in a straight line, but probably was originally formed for a detachment of Agricola's advancing forces.[5] The turnpike-road leaves the line at Four Laws, the Watling

---

[3] Hodgson's Hist. Northumberland, vol. i., Part 2. Near and north-east of this spot are some banks thrown up, like entrenchments.

[4] The position is advantageous; for, at a short distance north and south, a most commanding view is obtained of the line of road each way. The spot is called Swine Hills.

[5] There is a small camp about one mile and a half off easterly, on *Wanny's* Crag (*Dennis?*); it is about one acre in extent.

Street continuing straight up the moat, till it comes within about 200 yards of the summit of the hill, where it inclines a little to the westward, and passes close on the west side of some rubbish at a mine-shaft, under a stile. About here the road is still in a perfect state, a little below the surface, and a section of it may be seen where it has been cut through in draining. This bend, which runs along the summit of the hill, appears to have been made too great, and never altered; for when a sight is caught of the passage of the Rede, the road bends back again a little, to shape its course for the river. At this point the road is about 1000 feet above the sea, and from it the first view is caught of the valley of the Rede, and the whole course of the way to the Cheviot Range, the view of which is exceedingly fine. It is probable that there was a beacon on the neighbouring height, about 1200 yards to the eastward, from whence a view is obtained in both a northern and a southern direction. The spot is now occupied as an Ordnance Trigonometrical Station. The road continues nearly straight from the moor down to the river-side, and is best seen from the opposite side at High Leam. As it approaches the stream, it becomes indistinct, but its appearance on the opposite side, at Woodhouse, enables us to form an opinion whereabouts the point of intersection was. This point, probably, was near to where the river ran when the road was formed, and was the spot, perhaps, where the passage over it was made. Immediately before we reach the river, on the east side, we find the Risingham Station, the *Habitancum* of the Itineraries. (See Map-Sheet, No. 5.)

A map, on a large scale, and a memoir, is given of this place in the " Archæologia Æliana:"[6] it is, therefore, unnecessary to say much here; we may observe, however, that the area is 4 acres, 1 rood, 20 perches; the form a right-angled parallelogram, with the angles cut off by a radius of about 40 feet, and its height above the sea about 470 feet. The present state of the walls prevents any precise estimate of their thickness when standing, but from what remains they seem to have been about eight feet, built of rubble stones and mortar inside, and cased outside with good ashlar work. The side next the Watling Street is not parallel to it, but inclines at an angle of about 5°, and is, at the centre, about 150 yards distant from it. The gateway on the south, where the inscribed stone was found,[7] was probably the Prætorian[8] gate, for that next the road is not situated at much more than one-third the length of the west front from

---

[6] Archæologia Æliana, vol. iii., pl. 2.
[7] Thus explained at length by Mr. Thomas Hodgson :

Imperatoribus Caesaribus
Lucio Septimo Severo Pio Pertinaci, Pontifici Maximo,
Arabico, Parthico, Adiabenico Maximo
Consuli tertiùm, et Marco Aurelio Antonino Pio,
Consuli secundò, Augustus, et Publio Septimo Getae, nobilissimo Caesari.
Consuli,
Portam cum Muris Vetustati di-
lapsis, jussu Alfeci Senecinis (Senecionis ?) Vivi
Consularis, curante Antistio (or Anitistio) Advento pro
Augustis nostris, Cohors prima Vangionum—
cum Aemilio Salviano, Tribuno
suo, a Solo restituit.

Archæologia Æliana, vol. iv.

[8] Roy's Milit. Antiq. p. 49.

the north-west angle, which is about the proportion considered the best. Risingham station is 14 miles 2 furlongs from Corbridge in a straight line, and 15 miles by Watling Street.   The north front does not appear to have had any gateway, its resting on the bank of the river may have rendered it unnecessary; neither does there appear to have been any on the east front.   The ditch is of great width, about 130 feet: and though draining and local authority go to prove there never was any other rampart than the remains of that which faintly marks its outer boundary, analogy would lead to the supposition that there were two small ones.   If a line in the direction of the north front be produced westerly, about 150 yards, it will cross the line of the road close to where the edge of the river at present runs; and a few yards beyond, where (at a depth of four feet in the deposited mud of the river), the foundations of a bridge are said to exist.   This is so near the line of the road, that it seems probable a bridge was there; but to reconcile this, a very different course must be given to the river below the present bridge, or the road would have had to cross a second time; however, from the nature of the soil, and the course of recent changes, almost any direction may be assigned for the original flow of the waters.—(See Mr. Bell's paper in the "Archæol. Æliana," vol. iii. p. 11).

From Risingham,[9] the Watling Street ascends the hill to Woodhouse, passing under the front of the upper house, and, crossing the Crawden Syke, falls in with the present turnpike-road, and continues the same straight line for about two furlongs; here it changes its course a little, and passes about 25 yards on the east of Dikehead Cottage, leaving the public road at the turn where the parish road to Corsenside Church turns off.   At this cottage the way makes a new course, and is faintly visible by the west side of an old dyke, which seems to have been thrown up as a division between common and private land; and in about five furlongs meets the public road again, where the parish of Corsenside joins that of Elsdon.   This part of its course is by no means clear, for should the ridge which is visible be the line of road, it has been cleared of its stones for either making the fences or the turnpike-road.   What appears to be the line continues by the side of the present road, only it is on the *west* side now, instead of the *east*, and seems to have joined the present road again a little north of the two bridges, where it makes a new course; thence the

---

[9] "Risingham, *i.e.*, in the Old English and German language, the habitation of giants, as Risingberg, in Germany, means Giant's mountain."—Gough's Camden. It does not appear that the Britons ever occupied Risingham previous to the coming of the Romans, at least as a place of defence; there are some remains of walls like their residences on the Leam Hill, but no place of defence.   There was a beacon on Hareshaw, and another on the opposite hill, Hartside, but these may have been of later erection.   Camden and Horsley are the authorities on which Risingham is said to be Habitancum, from an altar found here dedicated to the god Mogon of the Gadini, on which *Habitanci* was inscribed.   On this word *Mogon*, Sir Samuel Meyric published some observations, in the "Gentleman's Magazine for 1828."   He says, "The British deity was addressed under the character of an ox or bull, whether considered as the leader in battle, as the supreme ruler of the land, or as the great object of dæmon worship.   The Druids, therefore, adored him in the image of a bull, or kept the living animal as his representative, and he was called Mohyn, or Möyn·Cad, and Tarw Cad, both of which signify the bull of battle."— Gent. Mag. June, 1852.   We received great assistance at Risingham from Mr. Shanks.

Roman and turnpike-road are in one for about five furlongs, when the latter turns north-west towards Troughend.  At about three furlongs east from this point is a small rectilinear and rectangular camp of about three-quarters of an acre, with one gateway only visible on the north side : the ground it is on is called Woodhill.  There is an unfinished part on the south, and it is probable that it has been larger, but no traces of such extension are now visible.[1]  The view from it is good; it was probably an exploratory fort.

Returning to our point, the turnpike-road bears to the westward, and the Watling Street continues straight towards Dun's houses, as has been proved by Mr. Thompson of Troughend,[2] in making a cut to drain the fields, when large flag-stones were found to form the road about a foot below the surface, some of the stones larger than a man could lift. Troughend lies about 350 yards on the west of the line, and is said to stand on a dike of whinstone of about 100 yards wide, with limestone on the south, and coal measures on the north; the dike may be traced in a course north-west and south-east, by a slight change in the vegetation, caused perhaps by the facility with which the water finds a passage through its fissures.

There are many traces of buildings about Troughend, which is an elevated spot, being about 800 feet above the sea ; and in the small garden at the west end of the house is a tumulus, on the west edge of which Mr. Thompson has seen squared stones taken out; they were forming the side of a square, apparently of about 15 feet side, and possibly, from the position respecting the Watling Street, may have been an ancient place of sepulture.  The road continues its course visibly by Dun's houses, where, having gained the highest part of its line, it makes the smallest possible change in its direction, and descends the hill towards the river, being visible in the field, at particular seasons, immediately below the Dun's houses.  About 450 yards from the buildings so called, the turnpike joins the line again ; the Roman Way, however, does not form the bed of the present road, but runs in a distinguishable ridge close on the east side of it.[3]  Arriving at the small brook at Dargues, or Duns (the name of two small farm-houses), we find on the north bank a Roman camp, seemingly hitherto unnoticed, and would certainly have remained so but for the name, *Dun (fortress)*, which drew attention to the locality.  The brook, and part of the land, is called Dargues.  (See Map-Sheet, No. 5.)

The camp lies principally on the west side of the Watling Street, its length being about 330 yards east and west, and its breadth about 220 yards north and south;[4] containing about 15 acres; one of its shorter sides being parallel to, and about fifty yards from, the Roman way ; faint traces of a gateway may be seen in the centre of the east front, and very

[1] The situation of this camp, and several others, was pointed out to us by Mr. John Arkle, of Elsdon.

[2] It is said that the ancient name of this place was Tre-hên, and the situation supports the supposition.

[3] Why the road was not more often taken for the modern way does not appear; unless it was a boundary line to be preserved, or, that the stones formed a convenient material to break up for the new line.

[4] The proportions of this camp are, in the opinion of Gen. Roy, that which Vegetius considered the best (p. 70).

clear evidences of one in the opposite front, with the usual inflexion of the rampart across the opening, but no trace of the traverse in front; the gate in the north front is equally clear, with its inward curve of the rampart, about one-third the distance along the front from the north-east angle. This seems to have been the only gate in this front; and we could see no traces of any gate in the south front, which is well defended by the precipitous bank of the stream. The camp is right-lined and rectangular. The south-east angle must have been where the turnpike-house[5] and garden now are; and an outwork across the road, extending to the edge of the declivity, seems to have been thrown out to defend the passage of the brook: these lines are nearly obliterated.

About 180 yards on the east of this outwork, and 90 yards east of the farm-house, are the remains of a stone ring, or tumulus, on a slightly elevated spot, rounded originally, probably, by the retreating waters, but having the appearance of artificial improvement; and on the opposite side the river Rede are faint traces of three other rings, which, as they are in a line nearly with Greenchesters, may be considered worthy of notice: it is conjectured they were tumuli. About 800 yards before we reach the river Rede we come to a camp, which, from being right-lined and rectangular, is presumed is Roman. It is on a rising ground where the turnpike-road makes a turn to the east to Elishaw Bridge. The place is called Brown Rigs, and the camp is on Blakehope Farm. The ramparts have been so utterly destroyed, and the ditch filled up, that it is with the greatest difficulty that the whole of the outline can be made out. It appears to have consisted of an interior area of about three acres; the sides being, as well as can be ascertained, about 130 and 110 yards respectively, and with probably four entrances, for the traces of three can be made out, and that on the west front retains faint traces of its traverse in the front; but what was the height of the rampart, or breadth of the ditch, it is impossible to conjecture, for the plough has been over it after it has been levelled. (See Map-Sheet, No. 5.)

The outer line of entrenchment has not suffered so much on the north as the other parts of the work, and here one of the ramparts, for a short distance, retains its height, with a ditch on the inside, as a defence to the other, which is nearly obliterated. On the east side this line is destroyed, and only the faintest trace can be seen of its existence. The same may be said of the south, but on the west a part still remains, but so much longer than the north front, that it makes the whole work look like a large encampment of 12 acres, with the inner one on the highest ground, and towards the northern side, as if it had been but the praetorium to the whole.

---

[5] The small property on which the turnpike house stands is called Dargues. " The form of the camp must depend on the nature of the ground; in conformity to which it must be square, oblong, triangular, or oval. It is esteemed the most complete, when its length is one-third more than its breadth; but the form alone does not constitute its goodness. The praetorian gate should either front the east or the enemy: in a temporary camp, it should front the route by which the army is to march. Within this gate the tents of the centuries or cohorts are pitched, and the dragons, and other ensigns, planted; and through this the soldiers are conducted to the place appointed for punishment, or execution.'—Vegetius, B. iii., s. 8, in Roy's Milit. Antiq. p. 49.

It is singular, also, that the Watling Street enters the entrenchment between the inner and outer lines of the west front, running parallel with them, which is unusual in this part of the country, and leads to the supposition that this exterior line has been a subsequent addition, to extend the accommodation for a stronger force than was originally stationed at this post.    Possibly a considerable force was required here to keep the Elsdon district in check; there is not a·very good view of the country from it, though it is not immediately commanded ; but about five furlongs to the east, on a very commanding height, overlooking both Elsdon[6] and the valley of the Rede, is a small fort, somewhat circular, though the sides are arcs of such large circles, that they would almost pass for straight lines, and give the character of Roman to the outpost.    It is between the farms of Shettlehough and Greenchesters, and probably has given name to the latter-mentioned farm.    It is cut nearly in halves by the boundary fence, as is sometimes done where the property is divided, having rights and title. by the holding an old castle or encampment.    (See Map-Sheet, No. 6.)

It seems there have been two ramparts, with a ditch between them ; and on the east is a small compartment, like the walls of a cottage and garden, which is worked into the rampart of the place, and conforms so well to the general outline, as to lead to the idea that it may have formed a part of the camp originally, and been walls for temporary shelter during its occupation. The area may have been about five roods, but there is little more than half of it remaining, so that it is not readily determined.    About 50 yards on the east are some stones pitched on end round a small space, like to what we have seen in other similar situations ; they possibly mark the place of sepulture of some person who died in the camp—it is on the Greenchesters

[6] The camp at Greenchesters appears to be one of a chain of earthworks, like British works, connecting Rochester with Elsdon, as suggested by Gen. Roy.—Milit. Antiq.    The moat hill at Elsdon is one of the most perfect entrenchments in the country ; that the Romans occupied it is proved by the altars dug up; one to Antoninus, supposed by Horsley to be Caracalla ; the other to a local deity, Matunus.—The Romans, perhaps, constructed the outwork round the conical hill, and may have improved its defences ; but it seems probable that the original foundation was British; that it was a place of worship as well as a place of defence, and that being a sacred spot, they, in imitation of their Roman fellow soldiers, may have made this altar to the presiding deity of the place, which the syllable *tun*, or *dun*, in the word may serve to confirm. Its present appearance reminds us of the Castle Hills at Catterick, on the Swale ; Sedberg, on the Rotha ; and Hornby, on the Lune ; which some consider Saxon or Danish works.    Those who look on these high defensive places as altars to the sun, may see in Elsdon the *Hauls-dun*,— (Brit.)—*fortress of the sun* ; rather than *Eld-dun,—old fort*, of the Anglo-Saxons. " That it was unlawful to build temples to the immortal gods, or to worship them under walls or roofs, was an article in the Druidical creed.    All their places of worship, therefore, were in the open air, and generally on eminences."—Mackenzie's Hist. View, vol. i., p. 18.    Possibly the same origin may be assigned to the Eil-don Hills, on the south bank of the Tweed, conjectured by Gen. Roy to be the Trimontium of the Romans ; one of them was a camp of some sort on the summit, though not so regularly formed perhaps as that of Elsdon.  " These very large hills I have often considered as temples to the sun, by a people the descendants of the Scythæ, whose religious rites are very similar to those of the Gentiles contemporary with the Patriarchs in Holy Writ.  They are found near, and sometimes within, the circle of our ancient castles.    That at Canterbury, called the Donjon Hill, evidently preceded the Roman station, the Roman wall passing over a part of its base."—Douglas, Nenia Britannica, p. 161.  Mem. Proceeding Arch. Inst. *Salisbury*, 1849, p. 298.

side of the wall. There is something like a road passing down towards Blakehope Camp, but too unconnected to be traced continuously. At the small bridge over the Dultr~~ brook, just before it falls into the Rede, are some banks on its north t ue, which look as if they had been thrown up, and the precipice scarpe ` dow ı to defend the passage; it is also said that the road over the Rede passed here at one time, but we see no evidence of it; or that there ever was any way ever here to Blakehope Camp, and Watling Street, particularly the way ment' ıd by Horsley.—(Page 26—Pref.)

From Blakehope Camp the ~~s of the Watling Street are still discernible across the moor, particularl at a fence about 170 yards from the river, which runs diagonally along it for some distance; but near the river it seems submerged beneath the accumulation from the periodical overflowing of the water. In the south bank, however, there are rotten small trees, and large stones evidently placed on them, so exactly in the line, that we are disposed to think them remains of the road, though now four feet below the surface. We may observe that had these trees been placed there to resist the destroying action of the river in times of flood, the wood would have been placed perpendicularly as piles, and not horizontally. Very nearly in the same line, in the bed of the river, and four feet below the lowest water in dry seasons, is to be seen (when the water is very clear) a piece of timber fastened down seemingly by piles driven on each side of it. A piece of this wood has been cut off and a table made of it, which has taken a good polish. It seems to be oak, and must have been where it is a very long time; for it is as black as ink. It is conjectured that this may have been part of a bridge at one time.

From the river Rede, the road is very obscure along the low ground, but we have traditional evidence that it was met with in cultivating the fields below Birch Hill and Bagraw, as far as the turnpike road from Horsley to Otterbourn, where the stones forming it may still be seen, on the north-east side of the road, where it has been lowered to improve the ascent. At this part it ran immediately on the west of an ancient entrenchment, which is cut through by the turnpike road, part being in the fields of Bagraw[7] and Horsley, on the west, and part on the waste land, and within the wall of the lawn before Redesdale Cottage, Mr. Lawson's residence, on the east. This camp appears, from a gateway and traverse in front and on the south side, to have been Roman originally, of about $9\frac{1}{2}$ acres, and nearly rectangular; and that subsequently the southern part had been added; for the gateway and traverse seem to be made in that line of defence which at present forms a division line running east and west through the middle of the work. The ramparts forming the south front are different also; the outer one having the appearance of being a banquette and parapet. Thus, it is possible, the entrenchment may have been extended by a sort of procestrium on the south, forming on the whole about nineteen acres. There is an entrance at the south-

---

[7] This name is sometimes called *Bograh*, and is so written in Horsley's Map; the latter syllable is British for *camp*. Mr. Fenton thinks it may be derived from *Bach*, *little*; and *Ra*, a *camp*. Perhaps the smallest Roman one in the neighbourhood originally.

east angle, and another in the north-west of the south half of the camp. From this camp the road is obscure, as it passed through the lands of Redesdale Cottage, close to the house on 'the west side, as we consider; for the plough has obliterated it at some e..tly period; and cutting off a part of the field above Horsley Inn, issued about 50 yards below the upper corner of the plantation above the church, and in a gentle curve ran past the tombs near Pettyknows, recently opened, on the east side of them, so as to avoid in its course all various inequalities of ground on either side,[8] reaching the station a Rochester (Bremenium) about 40 yards from the gateway on the east front of the fortress. The opening and description of these tombs[9] and tumuli does not fall within the object of this survey.

Nearly opposite Horsley, at a place called Evestones, or Evanstones, Mackenzie observes, " there are seven or eight Druidical circles or temples."[1] It appears to have been the site of one of those buildings known as Peel castles. There are many ruins of walls and buildings apparently, and the defences may have extended beyond the castle; but they are more right-lined figures than circular, and not much like those circles and upright stones we find in South Wales and Cornwall, supposed to be Druidical circles. The stones are large, and generally flat nearly, though in situ dipping gently to the south-east.[2] Camden observes, " Rochester, which lies nearer the sources of the Read, on the top of a crag, commanding an extensive view of the country below."[3] On which Mr. Hodgson observes, " On the east it is overlooked at a short distance by an escarpment of crags, and towards the south the ground is rocky and strewn with large, loose stones; but we could not find that the station itself was situated on a crag, as Camden describes it."[4]

It would appear, from a cursory view of the place, that between the " loose stones " at Rochester, mentioned by Hodgson—where the rock may be seen in situ—and the escarpment of seemingly the same stratum at Huel Crag on the north, that a great geological fault occurs, by which the rock which should underlie the station has disappeared. The whole is best seen from the west side of the Silloan Brook, where the line of fault, running up the meadow and continuing along the south ditch of the station, is very apparent; the little stream on the north of the station seems to be about the centre of subsidence, from some dislocated fragments to be seen near where it joins the Silloan Brook; and Huel Crag

[8] The manner in which the general line has been formed will be seen about 130 yards on the south of the tombs, where a curve is formed to avoid a ravine, and a fresh direction given to the road.

[9] The name of the spot near which these tombs stand is called *Pettyknows*, perhaps from the ancient British *Beddau*, *graves;* and the word *knolls* pronounced *knows.*

[1] Addenda, vol. ii., p. 486.

[2] Possibly a corruption of *Llech-faen*, *flat-stones*, which would apply very well.

[3] The name Rochester may be from *Hrof-top*, Anglo-Saxon; and *Chester*, a *camp.* " Richester in Readsdale, in Northumberland, must, I think, undoubtedly have been Bremenium. It stands directly on the military way called Watling Street, along which this Iter proceeds. The noble altar with the curious inscription on it that was found here, in which express mention is made of Bremenium, was the first motive that inclined Camden to believe this station to be it."—Horsley, Brit. Rom., p. 395. (See also Lewis's Top. Dic.)

[4] Hist. Northum., vol. i., part ii., p. 138.

may possibly be the extent of the disturbance on the north. The coal brought in by the fault has been worked, is very much shattered, and found not to be conformable to the general dip of the strata in the neighbourhood. The colliers are of opinion that this coal is that of a bed considerably above the one worked in the immediate neighbourhood; if they are right in their conjecture, it is probable there has been a subsidence to a considerable extent. On examination it will be seen, and probably from this cause, that the station originally must have been nearly surrounded by a morass, from water finding its passage through the lines of fracture. It is generally allowed to be the *Bremenium* of the Itineraries; and its situation at the foot of the mountainous district may account for its being so called, from *Bre*, a *hill*, and *Mynydd*, any *mountainous* uncultivated district (British); or from *Bryn-y-meini*, the *hill of the stones*—applicable to the district. It stands on a gentle declivity to the north, and contains about 4a. 2r. 33p., including the wall, which is rounded at the four corners by a radius of about 40 feet. The gateway in the west front is opposite to that in the east, and about 12 feet wide; they are not in the centre of the front, but about 28 feet nearer the north front than the south one.[5] (See Map-Sheet, No. 6.)

The north gate is in the centre of the front; and an opening like a sallyport, with a drain at the bottom and a footway flagged over it apparently, is opposite to it in the south: the opening appears to have been about three feet wide. The wall of the station, as now seen in several places, measures from 16 to 17 feet wide, but it is presumed that this breadth was not carried up to any great height. "A fort defended by a wall of ashlar-work seven feet thick, with ditches and treble ramparts." (Camden, vol. iii. p. 246, additions by Gough.) "It has had three earthen ramparts around it on the south-east; only one is now visible on the west and north." "In 1810 a strong tower in the south-west corner had some of its facing-stones remaining in their original position." (Hodgson's Northumberland, vol. i., part ii., p. 149.) The foundations of the tower here mentioned in the south-west corner are now covered up; but those of probably a similar tower are exposed in the south-east corner, which show the building to have been about 18 feet to the front and 9 feet wide, with walls about 3 ft. 6 in. wide. The front of the tower seems to have stood a few feet within the course of the wall. The foundation of a strong wall may be seen running in a northerly direction from the north-east corner; it seems strong enough for a wall of defence, and when compared with *Lindum*, in Plate 10 of General Roy's work, appears to have been a similar line run out to form a procestrium on some emergency. The two stations are not much unlike in size or defences.

Rochester station stands about 950 feet above the sea; is 8 miles 3 furlongs from Risingham in a straight line, and 8 miles 5 furlongs by the Watling Street. On the outside of the west front, at the distance of about 60 yards, is a round hill which has been called a tumulus; its

[5] From this it will be seen, that the north gate was the *rear*, or Decuman, *gate;* and possibly there may have been only a sallyport on the south or Pretorian front, which, from the nature of the ground, was the weakest side.

name is Gallow Hill : it may have been raised as a place of execution. About 110 yards to the south of the junction of the Watling Street with the eastern entrance, a Roman way appears to have branched off to the eastward ; the remains are very obscure, but enough exists to show that it ran close on the south of the farm-house called Dikehead, and on the north of the adjoining tumulus, proceeding over the moor on the north of an old lime-kiln.[6]

On leaving Rochester, the road makes a considerable curve in a north-west direction, to avoid the small stream, and crossing the Silloan Brook, where it is obscured by the deposition of the water, ascends the steep bank, and is visible again on the moor, maintaining a north-west direction for about 450 yards, where it shapes its course for the conspicuous tumuli on Thirl Moor, which are visible over the intervening height of Foulplay Head.

Before we proceed, it is necessary to mention two encampments mentioned in Gough's additions to Camden, " near Birdhope Crag, a little above Riechester, are two large square intrenchments, with two openings on each side, each defended by an outer oblong bank, six yards distant."[7] These entrenchments are one within the other, immediately opposite to Rochester station, and about 400 yards distant, on the Birdhope Crag ground. The exterior one, which being most submerged, and containing the peculiar inflexion of the rampart opposite the gate observed at Four Laws, we suppose to be the most ancient. The north side is totally submerged, and a great portion of the east side, except where a part seems to be preserved by the modern fence or dyke ; it may have contained about 25 acres ; it is right-lined, though not rectangular. The only entrance visible is on the west side—that on the south is too obscure to be certain about it. The inner camp is in good preservation—three of its entrances are visible, as well as the traverse in front, mentioned above as " an outer oblong bank." This camp is right-lined and rectangular ; is nearly square, contains about seven acres and a half, and stands about 130 yards to the south-west of Watling Street. Near these entrenchments are several low mounds, which have the appearance of having been burial-places ; but as none of them have been opened, it is impossible to say what they contain. The height of the moorland here is very considerably below the ground of Rochester station ; and though the Watling Street is visible enough near the camps, there is no appearance at present of any road of communication ever having been between them.

We now return to the angle of Watling Street, above mentioned.

Before we proceed from this angle of our road, it is further necessary to notice a large Roman encampment on a rising ground to the westward, at a distance of about three furlongs, extending over the whole summit of

[6] This information, and nearly all we received at Rochester, was obtained from Mr. William Coulson.
[7] Gough's additions to Camden, p. 246. " Birdhope Crag is situated near Feather-wood Burn, on the north side the Reed, a little above Rochester. Here are the traces of two large square intrenchments, with two openings on every side, each defended by an outward mole of an oblong form, at the distance of six yards from the aperture."—Mackenzie's Hist. View, vol. ii.

the hill, with its south-west angle resting on Bellshields Crag, immediately above the farm-house. Hitherto it has remained undescribed by historians, and is so much obscured by the addition of modern fences, as to have required repeated examination before the whole extent of it could be made out. The inflection of the rampart opposite the south gateway, is the strongest evidence of its Roman origin; but the line of rampart from this point to the south-east angle is, in parts, entirely effaced, particularly at the angle where the prolongation of the modern fence to the south prevents the round turn of the rampart being seen. Near the middle of the east front, which faces the Roman Way, traces may be seen of the gateway; but as the modern fence, with its ditch, has been run along the rampart, and is continued across the gateway, it requires close examination to see the traverse in front of it, the ditch of which is still well defined and preserved. About 60 feet to the north of this gateway, the modern fence leaves the rampart (which continues on, though nearly submerged in the wet ground, which wetness, it is presumed, was the reason why the fence was discontinued along it), and joins it again on the north front, about 260 feet from the north-east angle. The fence continues along the north rampart, though broken at intervals, but we were unable to identify any of the openings as gateways, from the want of the usual traverse in front. After rounding the north-west angle, we proceed along the west front, about 55 yards, where, at the distance of about 90 yards, is a spring, which, from stones placed along the line towards it, seems to have been paved. The rampart and ditch are here clearly distinguishable from the modern fence which runs near it, and obliquely towards it, from the north, joining it about the middle of the front. No gateway has been seen in this front. When we near the angle, a wall replaces the fence, and as it approaches the angle, the foundation stones may be traced conforming to the curve of the original work. This wall is continuous on the rampart at intervals, along the south front, to where the Bellshields property terminates, and Birdhope Crag comes in; thence, the rampart and ditch may be seen to the gateway, with the inflexed defence before noticed. The position of this camp is remarkably fine; it commands the view of the valley of the Rede to Four Laws; sees Thirlmoor, over Foulplay Head, and the upper approaches on the Rede; its extent is about 40 acres, and its height, above the sea, 900 feet. From a comparison with those in Gen. Roy's Milit. Antiq., it approaches the size and form of Kirkboddo,[8] and several others,[9] which the General supposed to be capable of containing a weak legion, with its auxiliaries. Should future examination bear us out in our decision, this camp may form some support to the opinion of General Roy, that Agricola advanced by this eastern pass of the Cheviot, with a portion of his forces.[1] (See Map-Sheet, No. 6.)

[8] " The smaller oblong camps in Scotland, which held between ten and eleven thousand men, but particularly that at Kirkboddo, which is somewhat narrower and longer than the others, is very similar to the camp of a single Roman legion, with its auxiliaries turned back to back, according to the Polybian system."—Roy's Milit. Antiq., p. 69.

[9] Gen. Roy's Milit. Antiq., plate 14.

[1] " He has supposed that General (Agricola) to have entered Scotland by this (eastern) pass."—Milit. Antiq., p. 117, note.

Before we return to Watling Street, we must draw attention to some ancient walls on the opposite side the Rede to this camp, about three quarters of a mile in a south direction.    About a mile above Rochester bridge, on the south side of the Rede, are two farms, called Birdhope and Wool Law. On the top of the hill above the farm-houses, are some ancient remains of stone walls, and an earthwork resembling a camp, which have much the appearance of being ancient British.    The remains of stone walls, which may cover about seven acres, seem to have been built with more design than for a village, and yet with scarcely sufficient for the residence of a chieftain.    The forms are generally quadrangular, with three or four circular figures, of 15 feet diameter, included within them, and having openings like doorways connecting the several compartments with each other; these stone walls are made of rude stones without any attempt at dressing of any sort, are of different thicknesses, from two to four feet, and generally about two feet above the surface, and in some parts so much submerged as to be scarcely visible at all.    Though near the top of the hill, they are not quite so, but a gentle fall to the south, for a few yards, leaves the surface occupied well drained.    There is a mound like a flat tumulus on the south-west, and several cairns of stones near, which may be sepulchral. (See Map-Sheet, No. 6.)

In Horsley's map of Northumberland we find the name of the ground written *Burdhope*,[2] and it is probable that its name has been taken from these ancient remains, and been *Berghope*, though there are no works of defence around them.    About 200 yards, however, to the south-eastward, on the most commanding part of the hill, is a small entrenchment, as a sort of look-out, or advanced post, having a most extensive view of the upper and lower course of the Rede, as well as the two valleys, Bellshields and Silloan.    The entrenchment, or camp, is rectangular, containing about ¼ of an acre, with two entrances on the east side, and with four circular walls within, similar to the circular compartments in the Birdhope remains, the centres of which are in line, and parallel to the east and west rampart of the work.    The ground on which this camp stands is called *Wool Law;* and it is conjectured that the adjective *wool* is a corruption of of the British *Wylfa*,[3] *place of watching*, and the *law*, so prevalent in the country, has been added since.[4]    Below these works, and midway between each of them and the river Rede, is a comparatively dry and plain surface, surrounded on the upper side by a rough stone wall and natural water-course, which watercourse, on each side, descends towards the river, terminating in a morass on either side where the wall is either submerged or has been considered unnecessary.    It is possible this wall may have been made for agricultural purposes, as the land enclosed, though in the middle of wood, appears to have been ploughed; but as a way from it to the westward appears to have connected it with the remains on Birdhope, and the camp on Wool Law, and the river with its marshy banks would have been a protection below, where the wall or rampart of stones is

[2] Also in Hodgson's Northumberland, "Burdhope Crag."—Vol. i., part ii., p. 149.
[3] Gwylfa, a place of watching.— Richards's Dic. Wilsh.

[4] These remains were pointed out to us by Mr. William Coulson, of High Rochester.

discontinued, it is possible it may have served as a retreat or defence to the places above.[5]   There are several cairns of stones within this enclosure.[6]

We now return to the angle in Watling Street before referred to.

Watling Street continues, as we observed, in the direction of Thirl Moor, but without any nice care to preserve the straight line, for in coming in sight of Featherwood, a slight bend is made to clear the waterfall, which could easily have been done without if desired.   On our way up the moor, however, before we reach Featherwood, we must turn aside about 400 yards to the eastward, to notice some remarkable knolls having the appearance of ancient tumuli, at a place called Petty May, on the banks of the Silloan Brook; these mounds appear to be natural elevations enlarged into three tumuli, the southern of which has a ditch round part of it, and gravel from the brook seems to have been used to construct them.   By the side of the stream below are three small compartments of stone, like graves, the most southern of which has a stone standing upright by the side of it.   It is probably a place of sepulture, and the name derived from *Bethau mais*, the *field-of-graves* (British).[7]   Proceeding on our way, we follow the curve of the road round the waterfall at Featherwood, where we find a heap of iron slag or cinders, probably of ancient formation, as the materials are coarse and rudely melted, unlike the cinders of modern times.   Crossing the small stream, the road forms a beautiful curve as it is seen to ascend in a northerly direction, to where the driftway turns off over the Broken Moss towards Elsdon; and where the boundaries between Featherwood and Redleys join.

This we presume is the spot where the Golden Pot stood, mentioned by Hodgson in his History of Northumberland,[8] as drawn in Armstrong's

---

[5] These works would seem to be of the same age as those at Colwell and Swinburne.

[6] "The Northumbrian Britons, though considerably removed beyond the gloom of savage life, were not very expert in the art of civil architecture.  We may readily suppose that some of the rudest settlers in this country, in the earliest stages of their residence, dwelt in thickets, dens, and caves, secured by art, and which protected them at once from the inclemencies of the weather, and the depredations of their enemies.  Even at the era of Cæsar's invasion, the usual habitations of the more civilised Britons of the south were very slight, and consisted only of a few stakes driven into the ground, interwoven with wattles, and daubed with clay, or covered with the boughs of trees.  These houses were circular, with lofty tapering roofs, at the top or centre of which was an aperture for the admission of light and emission of smoke.  Being constantly in a state of warfare, those erections were frequently crowded round the hut of their

chief, and defended by a ditch and vallum of earth, or else a rude wall of great loose stones, without either mortar or cement; while the entrances were defended by trees felled and thrown together in the most intricate and ingenious manner.  Such erections were generally built in villages upon the margin of a river, and sometimes on a promontory, difficult of access, and skilfully fortified."—Cæsar, de Bel. Gal., lib. v., chap. vii.; Diod. Sic., lib. v., s. 8 ; Borlase, Antiq. Corn., p. 292; Whitaker's Hist. Manchester ; Mackenzie's Hist. View, vol. i., p. 6.

[7] "It is wrong to suppose that the Britons were entirely expatriated from this district ; for as few women were brought from Saxony, the new comers, of course, intermarried with the natives.  This, indeed, seems completely established by the large proportion of the ancient British, and even some remains of the Roman tongues, which are mixed with the Anglo-Saxon dialect."—Mackenzie's Hist. View, vol. i., p. 55.

[8] Hist. Northumb., vol. i., part ii.

map.[9]  About three quarters of a mile further, ascending in a curve, we reach the summit of Foulplay Head; and on the *west* side of the road, at about 50 yards distant, we find the *east* front of a large Roman encampment, running nearly parallel to the course of the road, with an entrance in the centre, with a traverse in front, and that peculiar inflexion of the rampart noticed at Four Laws, and Bellshields; and similar in some degree to that mode of defending the entrance, exhibited in the camp of Dealgin Ross, in Strathern, in Gen. Roy's Milit. Antiq. (Plate 11), and supposed by him to have been the. method peculiar to the ninth legion.  This camp, though right-lined, is not rectangular; the northern front, which overlooks the deep valley called Cottons Hope, has two entrances visible, with each a traverse in front, but without the inflexion of the rampart visible, and seemingly never there; the N. W. angle is well rounded, and as the west front descends through the Moss, the traces are much broken and submerged, so that we could discern no evidence of an entrance.  The S. W. angle is in the lowest ground, where the water, kept back by the line of rampart, has encouraged the growth of peat, and occasionally broken through, carrying all traces of the line of work.  This will apply in some measure to the south front, which is broken through in many places, and we fancied we could trace the form of a traverse opposite one of the openings about the centre of the front, but as this would not be uniform with the north front, the existence is doubtful. (See Map-Sheet, No. 6.)

The area of this camp is about 42 acres.  The height of this ground is about 1500 feet above the sea: a most commanding view is obtained of the valley of the Rede, and the approaching line of road.  It is nearly flat at top, without the usual bed of peat and growth of heath which distinguish the heights which surround it; whether this barrenness arises from the nature of the rock below, which is said to be whinstone, or from the occupation of it by the Roman forces which are presumed to have been here, must be left to the opinion of the naturalist; but it seems probable that the ancient British, seeing this want of growth, would give the name *'Foel* (*bald*); and the Northumbrians, or Saxons, would add their characteristic name *blae* (*blue*), as distinguishing its colour from the *browner* heath-bearing hills which surround it; hence, possibly, may have arisen *Foulplay*, which, it may be observed, applies only to the hill, and is not the name of the properties over the summit of which the boundary line runs—Featherwood and Cottons Hope.  When this entrenchment is compared with that of Bellshields, each about 40 acres; and also with those in General Roy's Military Antiquities, particularly at *Kiethick, Lintrose*, and *Kirkboddo* (Plate 14), or with *Dealgin Ross* (Plate 11); it is presumed they will be considered the work of the same people, and calculated to support the supposition that Agricola entered Scotland by this eastern pass with a part of his forces.  (See Military Antiquities, p. 79.)  This

[9] Armstrong has placed the Golden Pots on the west side the Watling Street in his map; an examination of the ground, it is presumed, will show that they were on the east side, and so more likely to have been placed by the authorities of Holystone as Hodgson suggested.

entrenchment has not been described by historians;[1] and it may be worthy of remark that, being only two miles from the entrenchments of Chew Green, it is not probable the same troops would halt at Foulplay and again at a post so near to them.

The Watling Street is very visible nearly the whole way; and through the moors the ditch on each side would seem to have been increased in width, being full eight feet in most places, forming altogether a width of very nearly 50 feet. At Foulplay Head the Watling Street makes a slight curve, and directs its course to Chew Green. About 200 yards in advance there is a green spot in the Way, which, with the promontory running westwards from it, has the name of Calley, or Galley Knowl. About fifty yards from it easterly lies the inner Golden Pot, evidently not in its original position, which probably was the knowl in question. To the west of this Calley Knowl, about 250 yards, we find a round hill, called, in ancient maps of Cottons Hope, "burying-place;" we examined the spot we thought marked out in the map, but could not see anything satisfactory to make out the story. At three-quarters of a mile from this knowl, we reach the Golden Pot, which is the only one now remaining *in situ* of those mentioned by General Roy, and subsequently by Hodgson in his History of Northumberland; the latter's opinion—"that they were erected as boundary stones between the parish of Elsdon and the chapelry of Holystone, and as guides for the traveller in a high and very thinly-populated country"—seems the most likely account of their erection; and not that they were milestones along the Roman way. On each side the road here we observed old excavations, as if formed at the time of the construction of the road. This height is called Pepperside; it is about 1600 feet above the sea; and it was here for the first time we saw the *Noope* of the Cheviot shepherds, the Cloudberry, or *Rubus Chamœmorus*, of Linnæus; we could not find it below this height. The road here bends a little to clear the Cottons Hope Head, and ascends to the well-known height of Gammels Path, where it attains its greatest height on this side of the border, being 1640 feet above the sea. This name is said to be derived from the Danish *Gammel*—old.

Immediately above us on the east, is the remarkable and elevated conical height called Thirl Moor. It has probably been a beacon, from the extensive view it commands on both sides of the Border; and probably also a place of sepulchre, for there are the remains of three tumuli or cairns, on the top, and among the stones we picked up a piece of pottery. Its height is about 1800 feet above the sea, and only 858 feet below the summit of the Cheviot.[2] The ridge called Gammels Path, is formed by the meeting of Thirlmoor Edge with Harden Edge, and the fall to the Coquet is

[1] Unless the following comprehensive notice may do so: "The line of Watling Street in this parish (Elsdon) contains a chain of five Roman camps, and on the east of which line are several British camps, considerably more in number than the former, and all on the summits of neighbouring hills. Some of the Roman camps are less than two miles distant from each other."—Mackenzie's Hist. View, vol. ii., Addenda, p. 486.

[2] The name Thirl Mere occurs in the Lake District.—Sedgwick's Letters to Wordsworth, p. 53. Mr. Bruce says of Thirlwall Castle, "*Thirl*, from the Saxon *thirlian*, signifies to pierce, to bore. It is generally supposed that this stronghold derived its name from the Scots having

exceedingly rapid.   The name of this stream we suppose to be derived from the British *coch-red*, in allusion to the colour of the water from the peat, out of which most of it is drained ; in the same manner as we think the Rede to come from the same cause, the redness of its waters, and the Northumbrian manner of pronouncing the word red.

From the Golden Pot to the Coquet, the Watling Street is not clearly to be made out as heretofore ; and though it has been carried to the *east* of the Golden Pot in maps we have seen, we incline to take it on the *west ;* and, indeed, it is not improbable the Pot may have been in the centre. Descending from Gammels Path to the Coquet, the road has usually been taken to conform to the curve of the present road ; but we should feel inclined to carry it straight to the brook.   Four hundred yards above the Coquet we arrive at the extensive entrenchments of Chew Green.[3]   Chew Green has been generally considered to be the "Ad Fines" (from *Ffin— boundary*) of the Itinerary of Richard of Cirencester (see General Roy's Map).   It is 6 miles 6 furlongs in a straight line from Rochester station, and 7 miles 2 furlongs by the Watling Street.   The *most northerly camp* is a parallelogram of about 1000 feet by 650 feet, and contains about 15 acres.   The *central large camp*, which is nearly a square opening of about 990 feet each way, contains about 22 acres.   This large entrenchment, and the one before mentioned of 15 acres, appear to be the two most ancient, if we may be guided by the present obscure state of the ramparts, which in some places where the ground is wet, seem quite submerged in the peat.   The camp within this last, and the best preserved, occupies the western part of the height, and from its position, and the state of the rampart, seems to have been formed after the one on the east of it.   It is a parallelogram of 560 feet by 500, and about $6\frac{1}{4}$ acres.   In the southern gateway of this camp there is that peculiar inflexion opposite the entrance before referred to.   On the east of this last camp, and close to the Watling Street, is a nearly square rectangular camp, which, if it were not so close to the side of the large camp, might be taken as its prætorium. It is about 200 feet by 180, and contains about $\frac{3}{4}$ of an acre.   The interior seems to have been divided by an inner line or rampart, reducing the area to about $\frac{1}{2}$ an acre.   This is a very peculiar entrenchment alto-gether, particularly from the three surrounding ramparts,[4] the two inner of which seem to have been too small for works of defence, unless we take them for supporting palisades.   Altogether, the enclosure bears

---

broken through the wall here."—The Roman Wall, p. 270.   "It may, however, have taken it from the sluice or bridge where the river *passed through* the wall ; *thirl*," says Hutchinson, "being frequently applied to the opening left in moor fences for sheep to pass through."—Page 270. Thirlmere, in Cumberland, is peculiar for having a passage over a narrow part of it on a bridge ; hence, perhaps, *thirl*-mere. The pass called Gammels Path is where the Watling Street crosses a narrow neck connecting two elevated moors, *Harden Edge* and *Thirl Moor*.

[3] We received great assistance from Mr. Arkle, at Featherwood, shelter from the storm, and guidance over the moors.

[4] The whole distance of the three ram-parts, fifty feet, is not more than that of the first of three from the wall at Rochester.   General Roy observes of Chew Green, "We are rather inclined to place *Ad Fines* at *Chew Green*, as being close to the present border, and might even then be the frontier in this place between the Gadeni and Ottadini."— Milit. Antiq., plate 22, p. 117.

much the appearance of a religious structure, the more from a small building which seems to have occupied the middle, the foundation of which is still to be seen. A similar case occurs at Helston in Trigg. near Camelford, in Cornwall, which some have supposed to have been originally a pagan temple, surmounted by a christian building dedicated to St. Michael. (See Map-Sheet, No. 6.)

Immediately on the south of this camp, in the south-east angle of the larger, is a small one, the sides of which are not exactly conformable to those of the larger one, but nearly so; in extent about 270 feet by 180, and containing one acre. An attempt has been made to preserve in the drawing some relative strength in the outline of these and all the other entrenchments; but we have little confidence that it will be found sufficient, or any guide to the relative age of their formation.

Henry MacLauchlan.

BRADBURY AND EVANS, PRINTERS, WHITEFRIARS.

Ingram Content Group UK Ltd.
Milton Keynes UK
UKHW020052100623
423210UK00005B/137